S. J. GOSLEE

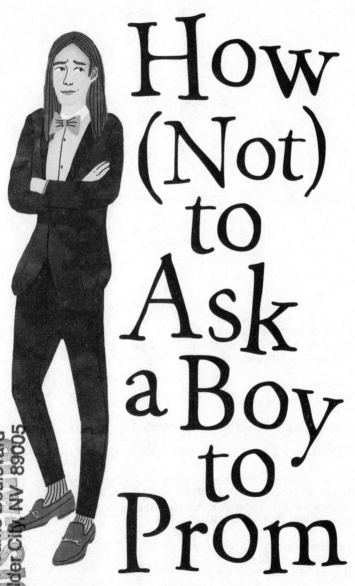

How (Not) to Ask a Boy to Prom

ROARING BROOK PRESS · NEW YORK

For Sully & Flynn

Copyright © 2019 by S. J. Goslee

Published by Roaring Brook Press
Roaring Brook Press is a division of
Holtzbrinck Publishing Holdings Limited Partnership
175 Fifth Avenue, New York, NY 10010

fiercereads.com

Library of Congress Control Number: 2018944873

ISBN 978-1-62672-401-3 (hardcover) / ISBN 978-1-62672-402-0 (ebook)

Our books may be purchased in bulk for promotional, educational, or
business use. Please contact your local bookseller or the Macmillan Corporate
and Premium Sales Department at (800) 221-7945 ext. 5442 or by email
at MacmillanSpecialMarkets@macmillan.com.

First edition, 2019
Book design by Aimee Fleck
Printed in the United States of America

10 9 8 7 6 5 4 3 2 1

One

Spring renewal comes with many things—the annual Sheffield Family Lawn Game Tournament, my part-time job at the Talbot plant nursery, an inexplicable increase in dick drawings on the outside of my locker.

What I don't expect it to bring, this year, on the day of the spring equinox, is my name being called in homeroom for the Student Advisor Program.

The Student Advisor Program is for juniors freaking out about college apps and the bored seniors who volunteer to help them. When my sister was one of those juniors last year, she formed a codependent bond in SAP with the co-captain of the golf team that basically weirded everybody out.

But me: I'm completely chill about college apps. I'm going to follow my sister to State, obviously, and if I can't get in there I'll probably just stay home and work for Mr. Talbot for the rest of my life. I've got a green thumb; it'll be fine.

Haimes says, "Nolan Grant Sheffield," and I straighten up in my seat, watch the other three kids in the class that apparently actually *did* sign up for SAP scramble out the door.

"Well, Nolan?" Haimes says, gesturing toward the door. "Report to the library. They'll have late passes for your first period."

"But I—" I cut myself off. Do I really want to argue about getting out of half of my gym class? We're starting a soccer section. I'm specifically exempt from the no-hands rule—lose a little blood from the face during kickball and apparently everyone panics—which will probably only give those jerkwads Plank, Sid, and Small Tony an even meaner edge to their play. I mean, they're pretty much the reason I always bleed in the first place.

I hightail it out into the hallway, preparing to explain to the librarian that this was all a mistake.

Maybe I'll take the long way down to the soccer field after I talk my way out of SAP. I can hang in the second-floor bathroom for a while if I have to, so long as Bern and his crew aren't monopolizing it for an organized roof climb—I'm 90 percent sure they have a rope ladder and a grappling hook hidden at the bottom of the trash can in the last stall.

At the library, I push open the doors and scan the scattered tables already full of pairs of whispering students and see . . . Daphne. All alone. Grinning, she waves both her hands at me and I palm my face with a groan.

Daphne Sheffield, graduating senior, my sister in all ways but blood: I should have seen this coming.

"You're joking," I say, dropping down into the seat across from her.

She's got out a notebook and a pen with a pompom on the end of it, a book on college essays at her elbow, and her grin is getting progressively sharper around the edges the longer she looks at me. Finally, she says, "I promised Mom I'd prep you for the SATs."

"You did," I say slowly. I fold my hands together in front of me on the table and try not to break eye contact.

Daphne has a scoop nose and wild dark ringlets around her head. There are deceptively adorable freckles along the tops of her cheeks. Her eyes are practically angelic, long-fringed, underscored with eyeliner, shiny with faux guile-lessness. She clasps her hands under her chin and says, "I did, baby bird. We'll even get you into some extracurriculars for your transcript, too." She arches an eyebrow. "You owe me."

"Oh?" I say faintly. I've got a sick feeling in the pit of my stomach.

"Game night. December," she says. "You owe me a favor. A boon."

Boon is such a broad word when used by my adoptive family. Because, as I've learned many a time since moving in with them three years ago, they're all competitive nut jobs. If Daphne hadn't forgotten about the promise she'd forced out of me—my head smashed into the carpet, caught red-handed stealing money out of the till, but god almighty we'd been well into our third hour of Monopoly, can anyone blame me?—I was at least hoping for maybe a servant for a week type deal, like when Daphne's mom, Marla, had to do all of Tom's laundry after tanking at Mario Kart.

I spread my hands out in front of me. "I wouldn't exactly call all this a favor."

Technically, to any outsider, this might look like Daphne is doing a favor for me. Technically, any outsider would be wrong.

Daphne reaches out and pats my arm. "Don't worry, baby bird. This is going to be fun."

Fun for Daphne is relative. Daphne likes pick-up games of basketball and watching shark documentaries and hanging out with Dave and Missy, who are the worst. Missy, in pale button-downs and sweater vests, wavers between being a hateful jackal and a sophisticated T2000 sent back from the future to murder all happiness. Dave wears flat-brimmed caps and hides his feelings in paperback books.

So I have my doubts about every part of this.

SAT prep, fine, I can probably handle that, but I know it won't stop there: Daphne is a hurricane.

Resigned, I pick up the book on essay writing and start to flip through it.

She slaps it down on the desk and says, "Hang on, baby bird, I have a list."

In English, Evie says, "What's wrong with your face?"

"What's wrong with it?" I palm my jaw and rub my fingers along my cheek.

"You're pouting."

I force my lips up into a smile, but I don't think it works.

"You were fine this morning," Evie says, suspicious.

I *was* fine this morning, even though there was a fresh penis drawn on my locker (large, and encasing both the top and bottom doors—I was suitably impressed).

And look, I got to skip most of gym! That's a point in Tuesday's favor, even if I had to sit through a bulleted list of all the ways Daphne thinks I'm doing my life wrong. I've been trying not to take it too personally.

"There," Evie says, stabbing her finger right in between my eyes. "You're doing it again."

"I have a headache." It's not a lie.

And then I notice that the seat next to me is filled with an actual body. That it isn't the empty void it's been for the better part of the year: a pale, institutional green chair paired up with a scarred desk that, if you look closely enough, was a hapless victim of my narwhal obsession. Weird.

The seat next to me in English belongs to Ira Bernstein, for the few times he actually decides to show up for class.

I'm not sure how he's passing, *if* he's passing. The only class I've ever seen him reliably attend is our art elective.

I've had English with him all year, and usually he's only in class when it's raining.

A glance at the window shows the sun shining, with only a few fluffy white clouds mingling in the blue.

I risk a full look at Bern—he's scowling down at his desk, and he turns to glare at me when he senses my stare. He's got the raccoon eyes of a sleepless night, and I can't tell if the redness of his eyeballs is from a bender or if he's been *crying*.

When he growls, "What?" I realize I've been staring for too long—*awkward*—and blink and look away.

———

It's all over school by lunch.

Metal Shop Gia and Bern were apparently one of the longest-running couples in our class, so their massive public falling-out and subsequent breakup is big news.

I feel bad about it for all of ten seconds, until Bern shoves me on his way out of the cafeteria. I stumble to the side and say, "Hey!" but all Bern does is grunt at me and stalk off down the hall, his shoulders hunched.

And then I feel bad all over again ten seconds after that. The room is buzzing with rumors about how Gia humiliated Bern in the parking lot before school. I shake off the odd feeling that I should go after him and—what? Offer a shoulder to cry on? A squishy body to punch? Bern spent all of freshman year low-key harassing me when I first came out, so we're not exactly on the best terms.

When I finally make it across the caf, I'm the last one to arrive.

Each and every person at my lunch table is technically one of Daphne's friends, not mine, since Evie refuses to drop French and switch lunches.

It's like staring at blank-faced, black-eyed demons for forty-five minutes out of every day, but they're the only things saving me from having to eat lunch alone in the bathroom or out back behind the auditorium, where some kids sneak off to smoke up and plot the downfall of mankind.

As I drop into the seat next to Carlos, Daphne greets me with another list. She says, "I'm starting you off slow," and I stare at her like she's a crazy person.

"Four hours ago, you shoved three SAT prep books at me." I resist the urge to add, *and gave me a point-by-point lecture explaining how I'm ruining my social life by sleeping too much.* And now she's giving me a list of . . . what, exactly?

She waves around the piece of paper. "It's just two things," she says. "I mean, how can you call yourself an artist and not be a part of the amazing and fulfilling Art Buddies program?"

Easily, I think. Art Buddies pairs teenagers up with kids

ranging in age from six to twelve. They're basically supposed to be mentors, and I have no business mentoring anyone that isn't imaginary or my cat.

Warily, I say, "You said two things?"

"The GSA is having a plant sale this year."

The GSA. The Gay-Straight Alliance club. Evie and I showed up once, at the beginning of our sophomore year, only to find ourselves surrounded by lacrosse jocks, cheer-leaders, Mr. Boater, and a massive number of feather boas, tiaras, and condoms. I never really understood what was happening, but Evie had grabbed my arm and pulled me out of the room before GSA President Si O'Mara—a god who was sent down from the Mount to smile blessings upon us—could open his mouth to even say, "Hi."

Carlos leans toward me and grabs my plastic bag of Oreos with a "Yoink." He stuffs one in his mouth and says around it, "Doesn't Evie have a rune tattooed on her hip to ward off the heebie-jeebies of the GSA?"

"That's a lie," I say. It's a patch on her book bag, but only because her mom wouldn't sign the permission slip for a tattoo.

Carlos shoots me a lazy finger gun and silently passes over his . . .

"Is this a block of cheese?"

He shrugs. "My mom was in a rush this morning."

I take it. I'm never really picky about food.

Daphne says, "Just think about it. They do public works! And they're always looking for art volunteers. I bet Parker Montgomery the Third has totally forgotten about that time you told him to fuck off."

I had totally not forgotten that time I told P the 3 to fuck off. There had been poster demands and I'd been in the middle of a stressful still life and it's not my proudest moment, but I probably wouldn't go back and change my response, especially since I'm 80 percent certain P the 3 still has no idea who I am.

And then Daphne tips her head back and sniffs and says, "Is it *meatball* day?" and I have to listen to her romanticize about watery red sauce for the rest of lunch.

———

In the afternoon I have my art elective, which I take because I'm some kind of masochist, obviously. Our art teacher, Ms. Purdy, is a sour old lady who thinks she should have been famous. She wears a constant pinched expression and clucks her tongue over everything I do.

Which is fine. I don't need her to tell me I'm awesome at drawing—I am, seriously—I just need her to not give me C minuses all the time, and maybe not act like Zamir Abadi is the second coming.

But what am I going to do, *not* take art class?

There's a big poster in the front of the art classroom of a smiling, gap-toothed kid covered in paint, with a sign-up sheet next to it, ART BUDDIES spelled out in puffy lettering. It's a constant all year—"New names are always welcome!"— and I stare at it with narrowed eyes and twitchy fingers. There's only about three months left before summer break. How much would this actually help me?

Evie nudges me toward our shared table in the back and says, "Don't even think about it."

"Daphne wants me to," I say, dropping down into my seat.

Evie rolls her eyes. "You have a problem. Daphne's not the boss of you."

It kind of feels like Daphne's the boss of me. I've never really gotten over that summer I first moved in with the Sheffields, when I was thirteen and impressionable and Daphne was really good at climbing up on things to give me noogies.

And now I have to think about the fact that Daphne's graduating and flouncing off to college. She's arguably my soul-twin, my one great platonic love affair—the keeper of all those dark times, when I was on the cusp of fourteen and terrified that her parents were going to throw me back for being defective. We've since moved on to greater things, like our shared love of narwhals and *Supernatural* and the double-chocolate cheesecake from Modeen's Diner, but memories like that stick: I was a wreck of hormones and nerves and foster woes, and Daphne showed me the brilliant weirdness that is the Sheffields' impossible yet possible life. We watch movies in the backyard and have family game nights and day trips to the shore that involve too many hotdogs and inadvisable amounts of time in the sun.

And that's all going to change. It's inevitable, like Grandpa Sheffield shuffling off his mortal coil and Waffle Sundays and the living-dead thing under my bed eventually burrowing out through my mattress to eat me. But just because it's inevitable doesn't mean I have to like it.

So. Art Buddies.

Flipping open my sketch pad, I say, "It could be fun?" Which convinces nobody, not even myself, that it could *actually* be fun.

Rob and Arlo drop down into their seats across from us at the long rectangular table. Rob says, "What could be fun?"

Evie says, "Fuck off," without any heat, because she has this knee-jerk hatred of Rob that stems from his codependency on Arlo, and how Arlo is the devil. Arlo *sculpts*; he has no business being that defensive of Impressionism. Everyone knows he just does it to piss Evie off.

"Art Buddies," I say, and Rob makes a face.

Arlo scoffs and says, "Good luck with that."

And then Evie has a silent stare-down with him that ends with her turning to me and saying, "You know what? Let's do it."

Maybe it isn't just today that sucks balls.

Maybe it's every day, given that they're inevitably all bookended by gym and chemistry. My lab partner in chem is Linz Garber. Linz Garber is a pyro, she probably needs actual help, but odds are nobody'll do anything about it until she burns the whole school to the ground. Dr. Carlisle gave me my own personal fire extinguisher for under our table two weeks into the school year.

The only awesome thing about chem is that I have it with Si O'Mara, the school's one and only openly gay football star. It's possible that I'm still not over my freshman crush.

It's possible that I've had it bad for him ever since he innocently helped me pick up my books and papers when my bag split open in the middle of the hallway between classes our first week in. It could've been a meet-cute. I had embarrassingly vanilla fantasies about sitting together in class, at lunch, hanging out at each other's houses after school—*Evie must never know about them*. But meet-cutes don't happen outside Hallmark movies that I definitely, absolutely don't watch. The only class we've always shared has been science, and we always end up on opposite sides of the room.

Today, Si has a flush to his cheeks, like he's been laughing. I slump down with my chin in my hand and catch myself in the middle of an audible sigh.

"Oops, crap," Linz says, and the distinct smell of lit paper makes my nose twitch. It's like—we weren't even *using* our burners, what the fuck?

I automatically flap my notebook down on her crumbling paper so fast Dr. Carlisle doesn't even notice.

Linz grins at me, sheepish. *Sorry*, she mouths.

I shrug—crazily enough, I'm used to it by now—and then shake ashes off my notebook and flip it open to a new page.

When the bell rings, I only stare a *little* creepily as Si packs up his books, scuffs a hand over the back of Mykos's head, and waves to P the 3.

Linz absolutely can't judge me for it.

And then Si's gaze sweeps the room and he catches me looking and I feel my face freeze up. This . . . has never happened before. His ice blue eyes have never locked with mine, like he's trying to figure out exactly where he knows me from, despite us both being right here, in the same classroom, at the same time, every day. Oh god.

His slow-dawning grin is blinding, and I'm pretty sure he means it for Linz; or for Steph Crane, who sits behind us; or for the happy, fluffy clouds floating past the far windows; but my mouth automatically twitches up to smile back.

And, okay, there's a burn on my cheeks that can probably be seen from space when Tasha Carmichael elbows past me to saunter up to Si's still-smiling face and hook arms with him.

Linz snorts and I mutter, "Shut up," under my breath.

———

Instead of immediately delving into the world of after-school activities, Evie and I silently agree to go home and sleep on it. At least that's what I think we're agreeing to. She doesn't stop me when I go for my bike, and I make my way home to watch *Ellen* and think about my life choices with my cat, Fuzzbutt McGundersnoot.

Fuzzbutt is completely unimpressed with me, in general, but he sleeps in my bed every night and is willing to rub his face on my face, so I'm sort of attached. He's a longhaired floofy thing, brown-and-white tabby, and both of my hands are buried in his fur as he tolerates an enthusiastic petting when Marla knocks on my bedroom door.

She leans into the doorframe and says, "I hope you don't think I'm meddling."

Lifting my head up from where I was definitely not making kissy faces at Fuzzbutt, I say, "Meddling how?"

Marla doesn't usually *meddle*. Tom meddles, because he still thinks he can teach me how to catch a baseball. He counsels grade schoolers and likes to analyze why I'm partial to plants (spoiler alert: they don't care if I sing to myself after hours at the nursery), and I'm pretty sure he looks at me sometimes and still sees the beanpole in worn Converse shoes they picked up in front of the group home almost three years ago.

Marla, on the other hand, has always respected my right to hate sports and own four different pairs of the same sweatpants and name every single jade plant I get Attila.

Moving into my room, she perches on the edge of my bed and pats my ankle. "I just want you to be as prepared for next year as possible."

Oh, yeah. SAP. I shrug. "Okay."

"To be fair," she says, grinning, "all I did was ask Daphne to lend you her prep books. So whatever else happens is completely out of my hands."

I muffle a laugh in Fuzzbutt's fur, because what can you do? Fuzzy flicks his tail over my forehead and then shifts over onto his other side, away from my face, but still within arm's reach.

"It's fine," I say. I don't know how fine it'll be when Daphne gets some real momentum behind her, but for now it's not so bad. Some studying, some after school Art Buddies shenanigans with Evie—I can handle it. Maybe.

Marla squeezes my ankle and then lets me go. She says, "Your dad's grilling steaks for dinner, and Daphne's out with Adrian."

I make a face, because *Adrian*, ugh. Adrian Fells is the worst boyfriend in the history of boyfriends, but Daphne is blinded by his lacrosse skills and shapely ass and probably his tongue, too. They've been dating since January. The only thing more terrible than Daphne dating Adrian—who has given me more than one bloody nose by "accidentally" tripping me down the school stairs—is that her best friend Missy agrees with me about it.

We shared a commiserating look of horror when Daphne announced their first date, and it was one of the strangest things that's ever happened to me. I hope to god it never happens again.

"Dad could use some help with the garlic toast," Marla says, and I sigh and roll up off the side of the bed and onto my feet.

Fuzzbutt jumps down, too, only he immediately disappears under the bed.

Marla says, "You might want to consider finding out what died under there, before it spreads to the rest of the house."

It's a heavy hint that I choose to ignore. Whatever is under there is starting to smell even stronger, and I really don't want to know what Fuzzbutt is doing with it.

Two

Because the high school lets out an hour before the middle and elementary schools, Evie and I have time to kill in between school and our first Art Buddies meeting. Which we are doing. For sure. It was touch and go for a while there today, but Evie's resolve solidified during art, after an offhand huff from Arlo. I'm almost entirely certain the aforementioned huff had nothing to do with our afternoon plans, and was most likely meant for Rob instead, and all the ways he was sticking markers up his nose. I'm not actually going to tell Evie that, though.

Evie's girlfriend, Tamara, is a junior at Holy Redeemer and works afternoons at the coffee and sandwich shop, Ground Zero.

Ground Zero has a hipster vibe, partly because of the Mumford & Sons playing quietly overhead and the stack of farm quilts for sale, but mostly because of the overabundance of actual hipsters, clad in scarves and ugly sweaters even though the temperature is pushing sixty.

The best thing about Ground Zero, though, is that two out of the four walls are chalkboards, and Tam's manager always lets us draw whatever we want. For me, that means octopods and narwhals and flowers. For Evie, that means her teacup yorkie, Peekaboo, sporting various fashionable neckerchiefs.

Almost all the hours out of every day, Evie projects an air of having it totally together. She's low-key disdainful of our peers, vicious at card games, and has extremely specific opinions on art, the CW, and Harry Potter. And then you get her within three feet of Tam and she completely loses her cool.

Tamara squeezes Evie's hand over the counter and Evie's faces goes up in flames, her mouth spreading into a wide, goofy smile.

Tamara says, "We have fresh eclairs and those peanut butter fudge brownies you like." And then she shoves a container of chalk at me and says, "You need to brighten up your face. Why are you frowning?"

I didn't even realize I was frowning, but now that she's said something I can feel the strain at the corners of my mouth. Ugh.

"Extracurriculars," Evie says with a roll of her eyes. "Art Buddies."

"Kids hate me," I say.

"How can they hate you?" Tamara looks me up and down. "You're like . . . a pipe-cleaner man, or a stick figure."

"Gee, thanks." I stick my tongue out at Tamara, hug my bucket of chalk to my chest, and retreat, leaving Evie to pick up our snacks.

We have a regular table in the back corner with optimal chalkboard access, saved from hordes of Kerouac-reading twenty-somethings by the meager natural light and lack of quirky-colored armchairs. It's a tall table with round stools that double as stepladders, so I can get nearly all the way up to the ceiling if I stretch. I busy myself organizing chalk colors on the tabletop, watching Evie and Tamara out of the corner of my eye. Tamara flirts like they haven't been exclusive for a full month, and Evie's shoulders loosen the longer she stands there, until she's resting an elbow on the counter and scuffing the toe of her shoe along the tile floor. She sends me a quick glance before taking the plate of pastries from the counter. Tamara grins after her as she walks away.

She's lost some of the giddy pink in her cheeks by the time she reaches me and drops the plate down in the middle of the table.

Evie says, "I'm going to need you to draw me an orca the size of this entire wall so Peekaboo can ride on its back."

"We have less than an hour," I say. I'm not opposed to drawing a killer whale, they're pretty neat. On the scale of sea creatures I like to attempt to recreate, killer whales are about a six. Not as many limbs as an octopus, no magical horn, but they've got big teeth and nice contrasting colors.

"Well, I'm certainly not suggesting we skip the meeting," she says, picking through the bucket to get to the brown and orange chalk.

"Sure you're not." I'm tempted to do it. Just tell Daphne I lost track of time. It's not even that big a deal, honestly, but I'd still feel guilty as hell about it. I sigh and say, "We're just going to try it. Once. And if we hate it, we never have to go back."

———

The Art Buddies program coincides daily with the elementary and middle-school aftercare and is hosted at the local community center: a giant, sleekly renovated building on the edge of town.

Following brightly colored poster board signs pointing the way through the building, Evie and I slink into the back of the large assigned art room at quarter to four. There's a sea of organized easels and art stations, kids grouped in clusters, and a vaguely familiar–looking stocky dude with a clipboard who waves us up to the front with a friendly smile.

We wade through a wide spectrum of kids and a surprising number of fellow high schoolers. I lock eyes accidentally with Bern, and then Zamir gives me a tiny nod of acknowledgment. I totally did not expect to see either of them here. It's possible I'm wrong, but I could have sworn they spent every day after detention hanging out in front of the Wawa with the rest of their friends.

Stocky dude's name tag reads ALLAIN with little hearts around it. He clicks his pen and says, "Cho and Sheffield, right?"

"Nolan," I say, and Allain nods.

"Sure." He makes a couple check marks on his paper, hands us some blank name tag stickers, then says, louder, "Newbies get the twins."

Half the room cheers.

Two dark-haired girls glare over at us in suspicion, like newbie is code for mass murderer.

Evie pushes up her sleeves like she's going to war.

I swallow hard and wave *hi*.

Mim and Bex are not actually twins. They're sisters, a little over a year apart, but they look uncannily alike anyway, with matching bobs and disapproving looks and only the very slightest of height differences.

Mim says, "Name," and then glares even harder at me when I say it. She's eleven, and I'm terrified of her.

"You have three names," she says, poking at my chest. "You told me three names, like you're a politician or an esquire or a *third*."

"Uh." I panic and back up a step. "Grant Sheffield is more like a hyphenation?" Only without the hyphen, but I don't tell her that.

Her expression only softens minutely. I'm not even sure it can be considered a softening; it's more like she's placing some of her intense hatred in reserve, for when I inevitably fuck up later in the day.

I flash a quick, panicked glance over at Evie, but she seems to be in a fierce stare-down with Bex, so no help is coming from that quarter.

Mim says, "I'm working with glitter today," and, "I hope you like dinosaurs," and it's like—who doesn't, right?

I nod meekly.

There are big tubs of pink, purple, and blue glitter glue, metallic markers, and a huge roll of construction paper at our station. Mim watches me like a hawk as I pick out a marker and arrange my easel, but it only takes a minute for her to dive into the supplies herself. She makes a triumphant *ta dah* sound as she clutches a box full of elbow macaroni.

I like sketching and painting. I've got acrylics at home, even though I prefer oils when I can get them. When I sketch, I use charcoals or soft pencils.

There's something freeing, though, in making a giant T. rex with a metallic blue marker. It looks lopsided, which Mim is obviously judging me hard for. Her herd of yellow-and-purple stegosauruses amidst a glittering pink sunset and macaroni hills is far superior, honestly, but I'm willing to look stupid in front of an eleven-year-old if it means she'll stop calling me Turd the Third.

At the end of the hour, Mim says, "Later, loser," which

is a definite improvement. She's smiling a little, too, so I'll take it as a very slim win.

Evie bumps my shoulder as she walks up with Bex, and I'm not at all jealous of the half-hug Bex gives her before dashing out the door with her older sister. Ugh.

"How did you manage that?" I ask, trying to decide whether to fold my dinosaur picture in half or proudly display it on our walk to the parking lot.

"She likes dogs and rainbows and making fun of Justin Bieber," Evie says with a shrug.

"There's nothing wrong with Justin Bieber," I say, because we've had this argument many times before—there is absolutely nothing wrong with Justin Bieber. His songs have gotten progressively cooler over the years, okay, and the internet is pretty sure he's hung like a horse.

Of course, Bern takes that exact moment to push past us toward the door, and I silently send thanks to the gods of pop music that I didn't voice that tidbit out loud.

Evie frowns after him. She says, "What's his problem?"

"Uh, everything? The world?" Maybe Metal Shop Gia really liked Bieber, and I've unwittingly reminded him of how she, so the rumor goes, told him to get fucked and die. That seems a little harsh after two years of dating, so I have serious doubts that actually happened.

"Cool dinosaur," Evie says, smirking at my picture.

"Damn right," I say. My dinosaur rocks, even if it has macaroni for teeth. "Wanna come over for dinner?" I feel the need to have some backup with Daphne. She's probably going to grill me on how not entirely terrible Art Buddies was and be totally smug about it.

Evie purses her lips and looks like she's waffling, but she'd be a fool to pass up an epic dinner at the Sheffield household. Tom's the best cook—I've witnessed Missy weep, *weep*, over his heaven-sent meatloaf, risking corroding her evil-robot insides—and there's a high chance of bread forts and/or little people made out of fruit. There could be an edible puppet show.

Finally, she pulls her phone out of her pocket and says, "I'll call my mom."

Sadly, there is no puppet show at dinner, but only because most of the kitchen table is taken up by a pirate ship made out of a giant watermelon. There's a dashing grape captain with a toothpick for a sword on top of a heap of cut fruit.

Tom doles out spaghetti onto our plates and says, "We had a first mate, but Fuzzbutt ate him."

Daphne kicks my feet under the table and says, "So?" She waggles her eyebrows. "How was it?"

"I made art," I say with a sweep of my fork. "And it's proudly displayed on the fridge."

"It's beautiful, sweetheart," Marla says, passing me a bowl of salad.

I straighten up at the compliment and beam at her.

Evie says, "The kids weren't that bad."

I don't exactly agree, but I don't disagree, either. I'm reserving judgment on Mim. Fifth graders are iffy: They're top dog now, and yet well on their way to the bottom rung of middle school. Her snideness may be all bravado, but she could also really just be a dick. Who knows?

Daphne nods like she's satisfied.

She tells Evie, "You should stick around after dinner. I found my SAT flashcards!"

"While that in no way sounds absolutely horrific," Evie says unconvincingly, "my mom wants me home before eight."

"Your loss," Daphne says.

Tom grins like a shark and says, "I want in on that action," because he's a giant competitive weirdo, and that's how, after Evie neatly escapes when dinner's over, we end up playing hard-core SAT-prep Jeopardy in the den, breaking not one, but *two* lamps and spilling an entire bowl of popcorn all over the couch.

Three

The end of March slips easily into April and spring break, and I celebrate a week of freedom from school and Art Buddies and the looming threat of other extracurricular activities by watching TV Land and painting.

I also ease into my shifts at the Talbot plant nursery on Monday, because we're still in the slow season. There are Easter plants to wrap in foil and the gardening store to manage, and I spend a couple afternoon hours rearranging the house plants. Which is fine, because I enjoy talking to all the new baby succulents.

It only takes me a few days to get attached, and on Wednesday, I smuggle home three of the newly potted ones. Mr. Talbot spots me, but he only rolls his eyes. I've been working there for two years, he knows me well enough by now. I've amassed my own little mini-succulent forest in the windowsill greenhouse Marla and Tom got for one of the windows in my room.

At home, I write names on their little terra-cotta pots in sharpie—Pete, Caroline, and Stanley—and Daphne walks in on me arranging them carefully in the sun.

She snorts, then falls backward onto my bed and says, "I'm bored."

"Where's Adrian?" I try not to sound snide, but it's not like she doesn't already know how I feel about him.

"Busy." She makes a face. "He can't even make it to any of the tournament."

Thank god, I think, because playing lawn games with Missy is terrible enough. The Thursday before Easter is the opening ceremony of the Sheffield Family Lawn Game Tournament, which this year will manifest itself as a screening of *Teen Beach Movie* and its sequel on the side of our house in the backyard.

I move Stanley and Attila the Second over a little, making sure to keep a path open for Fuzzbutt, who likes to drape himself over the top shelf. I lost many a plant to him until I learned to just leave room.

She says, "Missy's bringing a boy, though."

"A human boy?"

Daphne throws a paintbrush at my head, and I duck away with a laugh.

"Be nice," she says, but her eyes are smiling. "He's got a nose ring and he shaves his head, Nolan. They fought over pretzel bites at the movies yesterday. It was the most precious thing I've ever seen."

I'm skeptical. Not much about Missy Delgado can be called precious. The closest thing to a good side Missy has is an entirely separate person—her cousin, Carlos.

There has to be something wrong with this guy, but at least he'll make our teams even.

———————

By 8 p.m. Thursday, Tom has the makeshift movie screen set up, and Marla has reorganized all the loungers and chairs on the patio. They're all pushed together and covered with blankets and pillows and the occasional TV tray. I've made a butt-load of popcorn with the air popper, and Daphne's filled a cooler with soda and juice. Tom's just about done setting up the projector when Missy and her date arrive.

Gator—*Gator?*—is bald, freshly shaved, and wearing tight pants and thick black glasses. The tattoo on his neck, in the dying light, looks like an electric blue tarantula. He holds Missy's hand like she's something fragile and not a sophisticated AI with secret plans to wipe out the human race.

I can't help staring. She's wearing a *peasant blouse*. There are tassels on her flats, and she smells like magnolias. It's fucking with my head.

I accidentally step too close and Missy twists a vicious pinch into the back of my arm, hissing, "Not one word, asshole."

Tom ignores us with a polite, "How did you two meet?"

Daphne jumps in, "He's in a band." Both of her palms are pressed to her chest, like she can't believe how adorable Missy and Gator are, sitting on a rattan settee in the middle of our makeshift backyard theater. "They met at the skater park. It was a *dream*."

Missy glares at her and mouths *I will kill you*, but Daphne just grins brighter.

I watch as Gator squeezes Missy's hand and says, "There was a sixty percent chance I was gonna get punched when I asked for her number, but I decided to go for it anyway."

"Oh, that's sweet," Marla says, bemused.

Missy says, "It wasn't that bad," and Gator says, "I think you called me a dickhead in Spanish," but he's grinning at her.

It looks like Missy is blushing. "You nearly ran me over!"

"Can we start the movie now?" I'm not sure I can handle Missy acting like a fully functioning human being. I've tried to make nice with her before. I know it's a sore spot with Daphne that we don't get along, but it honestly isn't my fault.

It's just that Missy can be a soulless, rabid hellhound.

Standing in front of the white sheet clipped up against the house, Tom claps his hands together and says, "Welcome to the second annual showing of *Teen Beach Movie*, now with bonus *Teen Beach 2*. Feel free to join in on the dance sequences!"

Marla and Daphne clap and shout, I sink down lower in my seat, and Gator says, "This is gonna be awesome."

I'm not sure if "awesome" is an accurate description—I like to reserve that for Captain America nights, or our Halloween horror extravaganza—but I appreciate the beach theme for an early kickoff to summer, and the way Tom gives us sheets of lyrics.

Tom and Marla barely make it all the way through the second movie. They're up in bed by midnight, probably already sound asleep.

Missy and Gator are sitting side by side at the patio table arguing about, I'm pretty sure, the probabilities of time travel. The Blu-ray projector is on a constant loop of dancing teens, but we turned the sound off a while ago, once the songs went from campy to just plain grating.

"I'm going to miss this," Daphne says, curled into my side, our loungers pushed together.

She sniffs a little and tugs a blanket up further onto our laps. The night has gone past cool, I've got my hood up, and there's a light breeze rustling the leaves of the two big oaks in the yard. The crickets are just starting to get a little noisy for the season. The sky is cloudless, stars bright, moon big and pale.

I don't say anything. I'm going to miss this, too.

And then she ruins everything by sitting up and saying, "You need a high school musical, Nolan! You need to sing and dance your way through senior year with a guy who will

drop you like a hotcake for college and then you can fuck
your way through your dorm—"

"I don't think that's how *High School Musical* actually
goes, Daph," I say dryly.

Gator is looking at me in fascinated horror, like he
can't believe this conversation is happening, but he kind of
wants to hear more.

Missy bares her teeth and says, "Good luck finding
someone willing to touch you, Grant," and Daphne slaps a
hand over my mouth before I can reply with something
equally shitty.

She keeps her arms around me and expounds on all the
ways I can milk a broken heart with older men. I'm just
really happy Tom and Marla aren't still there to hear it.

Later, when Missy and Gator have finally left, as we're
cleaning up the yard, stacking popcorn bowls and tossing
all the paper cups and napkins in a trash bag, Daphne says,
"Tonight was good, right?"

There was an embarrassing sing-along earlier. I don't
know if I've ever laughed so hard in my life when Tom and
Gator got Missy to dance.

"Yeah," I say. "Tonight was okay."

The Sheffields are a competitive bunch to begin with. Tom
and Daphne have a notebook full of tallied wins and losses

that goes back at least ten years. Marla is usually the reigning Scrabble queen. She likes to pretend she doesn't lock herself in the bathroom with a glass of wine when she happens to lose—she calls it "taking a bath" but we all know better. Risk is a road to hell that *nobody* wants to travel down anymore.

But add in some horseshoes and Baggo and it gets downright ugly.

Midmorning on Friday, Missy shows up at our house with Gator again and two jugs of lemonade. I get Tom in the partner pickings, and Daphne ends up with Missy since Marla wants a crack at the newbie.

We start easy, with bocce ball. No one gets hit in the head—Tom, last year—or starts crying—embarrassingly, me, almost every year—and Marla and Gator manage to eke out a too-close win.

Next up is croquet on the front lawn, which segues into horseshoes in a neighbor's pit, Baggo under the old tree house, and a finale featuring Missy and Daphne beating the pants off everyone in archery—mainly because the sun is shining so blindingly above us, it's making it hard to properly see the target, but also because everyone else sucks.

"Who decided to add archery this year?" Tom says, pouring lemonade while the waffle iron heats up.

"You did," Marla says. She kisses his temple and pats his back in mock sympathy.

We dig out the ice cream and everyone gets a bowl while

Tom fashions a tower of waffles for Daphne and Missy, their well-earned trophy. He slides it over to them on the table with a flourish. It's topped with syrup and even more ice cream, and I know from experience—Tom had been tackled viciously for stealing the waffles last year—that no one gets to share.

"Man, you guys are awesome," Gator says over his bowl of chocolate and strawberry ice cream. "Missy's dad hates me."

Missy cuts off a giant piece of waffle and says, "He doesn't hate you, he just thinks you should have a name other than Gator," before stuffing the entire thing in her mouth.

"Your parents actually named you Gator?" I ask.

"My parents named me an abomination," Gator says, "and I really liked reptiles when I was a kid."

Missy swallows her bite and says, "Carlos likes you."

"Carlos likes everyone except his ex-girlfriend and Eli Manning," Daphne says, which is true. Carlos has evil-twin theories despite the Mannings' age difference, and his ex-girlfriend is the devil.

Tom pats Gator's back companionably. "It's okay, you'll always be welcome here. Unless you hurt Missy," he says, "and then no one can save you."

Marla nods. "Remember, I'm a doctor. I can make it seem like an accident."

Gator looks like he's not sure whether to believe them

or not, and I duck my head over my bowl of ice cream and grin.

———

While none of us are particularly religious, candy and Easter egg hunts are a big deal.

And by "a big deal," I mean huge spectacles of enforced public embarrassment. It's usually best to go into a candy coma and wake up Monday morning with a limited memory of the shenanigans.

This particular Easter, we crash the local Presbyterian church's outdoor sunrise service—it's cold, and Daphne and I fall asleep on each other halfway through—and then head over to Missy's house for a hearty breakfast with the Delgados and a cutthroat game of Find the Three-Pound Chocolate Rooster.

I sit in the corner of the kitchen for most of it. It's not that I don't want to find a three-pound chocolate rooster, or any of the many eggs that go with it, but it's 8 A.M. and my body hasn't figured out how to work properly yet. I blink blearily at my enormous plate of scrambled eggs and try to remember why I thought I could force anything down this close to dawn. I've been up since five and I want to die.

Carlos sits down across from me with a plate of something cheesy and salutes me with his fork.

I hear the delighted screams of children, Daphne, and

Tom through the open window and push my plate far enough away so that I can lay my head on my arms on the table.

"Do you think they found the chicken?" I ask through a yawn.

Carlos shrugs and says, "It was my job to hide it this year."

I wait for him to explain, but he just shoves eggs and bacon in his mouth and stares me down.

I say, "So . . . let me guess, you didn't actually hide the chicken?"

Carlos just takes another bite and grins.

It takes three hours for everyone to realize the three-pound chocolate rooster is under Missy's bed. Missy is silent and coldly furious watching all the little kids gleefully tear her room apart. Tom eventually ends up standing in the middle of her mattress with muddy shoes on, chocolate rooster raised in triumph.

Daphne hugs Missy around the neck and says, "Don't be such a downer, Swiss Miss. I'm gonna share all my jelly beans with you," as Tom leads all the little kids through a rousing rendition of "Here Comes Peter Cottontail."

All in all, it's not the absolute worst way to end spring break.

Four

Adrian Fells breaks up with Daphne early in April and is a giant douchebag about it to the surprise of almost no one.

On the one hand, I'm relieved, because who honestly liked Adrian? Adrian Fells is a monster. If I thought I could get away with it, I'd run over him repeatedly with my ten-speed. Everyone knows that Adrian Fells is a monster, but he's also captain of the lacrosse team and his family has more money than the Catholic god. Adrian has a slick, greasy side for everyone that isn't considered a loser.

On the other hand, Daph is devastated, because she somehow actually liked the asshole and was one of the few people who didn't think he could ever possibly be a giant dick. Go figure. It's upsetting to see her like this.

On the other *other* hand, this increases her interest in my life by tenfold, and she really had way too much investment in it to begin with. Daphne decides to forego her usual post-breakup ritual—scrapbooking, video splicing, obsessive fanfic writing, sewing little superhero outfits for Fuzzbutt—and turns me into her main project instead.

Just two days after her breakup with Adrian, Daphne weasels her way into my room with a hopeful expression and what looks suspiciously like a joint Junior-Senior Prom ticket. She sizes up my cut-off, paint-splattered sweatpants with a, "We can work with this."

"What?"

"You're almost seventeen, baby bird, time to fly out of this nest." She makes an expansive gesture, the flap of her hand taking in my unmade bed, piles of clothes—I have them organized by both scent and season—and the precariously balanced manga on my desk.

"I'm not sure what you mean." I say this both as a stalling tactic and because I'm not actually sure what she means. I edge toward the door, hoping she won't notice I'm about to make a run for it.

"Nolan," she says, "have you, or have you not ever been kissed? Have you been on a *date*?"

I scowl at her. She already knows the answers. It's not exactly like Penn Valley is brimming with prospects, and I spend all my free time with Evie or plants.

"Here's the deal," she says, stepping closer to me. She pokes me in the chest with what I can see is *definitely* a Prom ticket now.

I say, "No," faintly horrified. She can't mean what I think she means. She *can't*.

"I'm not letting my forty bucks go to waste because Adrian's a dick—"

"Is that *your* ticket? Can't you just go by yourself?"

"That's exactly something I do not want to do," she says, still poking me. "Your date choices are Mykos or Si." I open my mouth to—protest? Gasp my last breath and die?—and she adds, "Those are you *safest* choices. There's always Hot Todd at the Wendy's or one of your art class randos, but there's a higher probability of rejection there."

"And you think there *isn't* with Si O'Mara?" I ask, appalled. I don't even bother mentioning Mykos. Mykos took a sock puppet to Homecoming. He's an enigma wrapped in a puzzle swallowed by a fuzzy turtleneck with a picture of a Ritz cracker on the front. That is the exact outfit he's been wearing at least once a week for the past three years.

But Si O'Mara doesn't even know I'm alive. A shot of terror zips down my spine at the thought of asking to borrow a pen from him, let alone asking him out. I can just imagine his blank look of *who the fuck are you?*, even as he politely lets me down easy. There is no world in which Si O'Mara would say yes to me—a date, a pen, sucking face in the broom closet. Holy fuck, my face heats up in embarrassment just thinking about it. Hands shaking, I say, "No," again.

Daphne grasps my chin, tilting my head down and looking into my eyes. She says, "Baby bird, what aren't you telling me?"

"Absolutely nothing." If she doesn't already know about my massive, debilitating crush on Si, I'm not going to mention it ever.

She tries to wait me out, but I keep my mouth zipped shut.

Finally, she says, "We're gonna make this work. You really should join the GSA."

I grimace. I'd hoped she'd forgotten about that.

She clucks her tongue. "I have no problem helping you out, okay? You need me to put in a good word with Si or Mykos, I totally will."

"How is that helping me out?" I ask. How in any world would that be considered *helping me out*, oh my god. And, also, "How do you know they don't already have dates?"

"Mykos is currently going stag with Wart and Aaron, and I have it on good authority that Si is Tasha Carmichael's backup date, in case no one else asks her—"

I can't imagine a world where Tasha Carmichael needs a backup date; she was the freaking Homecoming queen two years in a row and has extremely white teeth, dimples, and a forehead that works with bangs.

"—so I'm giving you a week before I make the choice for you."

"I'm sorry, what?" I couldn't have heard that right.

"They're both nice guys; it'll be fine."

I'm pretty sure she's joking. She's grinning like she's on the last thread of her sanity, though. Like Adrian has pushed her to these extremes. Like it's either set me up with a dude or she'll have no choice but to eat an entire extra-large pizza by herself, sobbing. But . . . "You can't actually do that, you realize that, right?"

She takes both my sweaty, anxious hands in hers, squeezes my fingers. "You're leaning toward Si, I can feel it."

She can feel my panicked heart battering against the inside of my chest. "No," I say.

"First," she says, ignoring me completely, "do you have any jeans that actually fit?"

———

The next few days fly by in a blur of uncomfortable pants and extracurricular activities. I'm trying this thing where if I believe hard enough, everything I don't want to do will just fade away into nothingness. So far it isn't working.

Daphne quizzes me every morning on words I'll never remember, I get two minor head wounds in gym, and Ms. Purdy gives me a C minus on a still life of squash. *Squash*, arguably the quintessential vegetable for a still life: lumpy, lopsided, round, colorful. I regularly complain about how much I hate still-life drawing, but to get a C minus on one that is considered on the *lively* end of inanimate is a tragedy that can only be explained by how much Ms. Purdy hates me as a person.

Every time I see Si in the halls or class—smile beaming, long fingers tucked into the straps of his backpack, tight jeans showcasing the thighs of a gladiator—I lock up, my entire body burning with adrenaline and fear.

The only bright spot is Art Buddies, which has become no less chaotic, but Mim has apparently decided to put up with me.

By Thursday we've settled into a regular place between Bern and a kid whose nametag reads KIP, who has a thing for seashells and rubber cement. Bern's partner is a chatty preteen with enormous hair and an even bigger smile. It's surreal seeing them high-five, but every time Bern catches me looking at them, his expression dips into intense scowling: a silent warning to keep my nose out of his business, or maybe he'll have to keep it out *for me*. With his fist. He's got dark, tired eyes, though, his face is pale, and there's a smudge of blue paint across his forehead.

Mim clears her throat pointedly and says, "I should set you up with my cousin," like she can sense my impending doom by way of Prom and my sister.

"How are you eleven?" I say, looking down at her.

"Nearly twelve." She gazes at me with a speculative gleam in her eyes. There are specks of glitter all over her hair and what looks like expertly applied eye makeup. She says, "I'm trying to figure out how your heights match, and if your mouths will line up."

"I'm uncomfortable with this," I say as I feel my face turn hot.

Mim says airily, "I know."

"Also, I'm, uh," I spin my marker between my fingers, almost fumbling it, "gay."

Mim says, "I know, duh," and finally goes back to her drawing.

I'm left to assume that Mim's cousin is a guy, and I fight the urge to cover my face with both my hands. This is the most awkward conversation I've ever had with an almost-twelve-year-old.

"I don't need you to set me up with your cousin," I say. It'd probably be only slightly less of a disaster than being forced to ask out Si O'Mara.

Mim squints up at me. "Well," she says, drawn out, like she thinks I'm being stupid about this, "if you change your mind."

"I won't," I say. I already have Daphne breathing down my neck. I don't want a kid I barely know telling me I need to date, too.

Mim flicks her fingers at me and then goes back to her actually pretty excellent field of Galloway cows.

I've been mindlessly pasting cut-out circles on a red piece of paper, but when I really look at it, it turned out kind of cool. I sign it in the bottom right with a flourish and then it's time to go.

Evie gives Bex a giant hug when they reach our station.

Mim slaps my side in what I choose to believe is affection before linking arms with Bex and dragging her out the door.

"I don't entirely hate this," Evie tells me.

"That's because you didn't get the evil twin," I say, swinging my backpack over my shoulder. I try for a convincing grin, but she narrows her eyes at me.

"All right, spill," she says. "You've been acting strange all week."

I sigh, glance at the sky, and briefly pray for the earth to open up and swallow me. Finally, I say, "Daphne may or may not be making me ask someone to Prom."

———————

"If I ignore it, it's not happening," I say.

"That doesn't even work for ostriches," Evie says.

We're at the back of the Wawa, trying to decide between smoothies and milkshakes. I push the button for chocolate.

Evie slams a cup under the raspberry smoothie machine and says, "Daphne always does this to you."

"She doesn't," I say. Daphne's always looking out for me.

"P the 3's pool party last year."

I hunch my shoulders a little. "Pushing me into the deep end isn't the same thing."

"You didn't want to swim," Evie says. She tops off the smoothie with whipped cream. "She has no boundaries with you. You refuse to give her boundaries!"

I pick up a soft pretzel and eat it while we wait in line at the checkout.

Evie pokes me in the middle of the back and says, "You can tell her no sometimes, you know."

"I can tell her no, but that doesn't mean she'll actually listen."

"Boundaries," Evie grumbles.

Outside, the sun is low and blindingly orange, setting the tree line on fire. I've probably just ruined my dinner with the pretzel and this milkshake, but I take another long slurp of it anyhow.

Five

Friday morning happens.

The day of judgment. My Prom date deadline, before Daphne takes the fate of my high school life into her own hands. Her room is unnaturally quiet as I tiptoe past it and into the bathroom.

I hum nervously as I pull my hair back into a rubber band and scrub my face. Blinking water out of my eyes, I flatten my palms on either side of the sink and stare at my reflection. I can do this. I can ask out Si. Or Mykos. Groaning, I squeeze my eyes shut and lean my forehead into the mirror. This is going to be a nightmare.

Heaving a deep breath, I straighten up, tug my T-shirt down, and attempt to fix my ponytail before shrugging it off as a lost cause.

Having fully brushed and neat hair is not going to help me. The only thing that's going to help me is the Rapture, and odds of that happening this morning are, like, a million to one.

Sneaking past Daphne's room again, I slip downstairs, grab three pieces of toast off Marla's leftover breakfast plate, and shove the banana Tom wordlessly holds over his head into my book bag, along with the paper-bag lunch with NOLAN written on the front in red sharpie.

At the kitchen table, Tom looks up from his iPad and arches an eyebrow at me. He says, "Your sister's already up and gone—"

Oh no.

"—do you have any idea why that is?"

I have plenty of ideas, none of which I'm telling Tom.

Daphne only gets out of bed early for a few reasons: One, she never went to bed the night before (but she fell asleep on the couch last night, and Tom and I had to practically carry her up the steps). Two, field hockey practice (but the season ended before Thanksgiving). Or three—anything to do with torturing me. Over the summer, some days she'd get up just to drive me to work by way of Wendy's and Hot Todd, so she could flirt really badly with him on my behalf. I only put up with it because, uh, Hot Todd is both hot and fortunately oblivious to terrible flirting.

My hands start to sweat, and I wipe them on my sweatpants.

I say, "No clue."

"Right," Tom says, amused. "Sure. Fair warning, though, she had *crafts*."

———

There's no sign of Daphne at school when I get there. No flash of her in the hallways between homeroom and gym. I stop by my locker before English for my forgotten Pygmalion book and nearly jump out of my skin when someone clangs open their own five lockers down from me.

I'm having a Daphne-related nervous breakdown.

It's almost a relief when I finally run into her in between classes, as I'm heading down the art and lifestyle wing to cut through the courtyard for history.

"Nolan," she says, appearing out of the sea of students with a manic smile and taking a firm grip on my arm, "excellent timing. Come with me."

"I have history," I say, trying to inch backward and wiggle my arm out of her hold.

"History is crap and lies," Daphne says absently, dragging me down to where I can see Missy at the end of the hallway.

Missy is holding a box with streamers spilling out of it, an evil twinkle in her eyes. She's not quite smiling, because smiling would require a certain level of happiness that Missy would never be able to achieve while looking directly at me. But she seems abnormally pleased, and all sorts of alarm bells start ringing in my head.

"What?" I say, digging my heels into the linoleum. The rubber of my sneaks catches and squeals and almost makes me fall on my face.

"This is for the best," Daphne says.

I open and close my mouth, throat dry with nerves. "Daph—"

Missy deadpans, "I added all the glitter," and a little piece of my soul dies.

We're five doors down from the home ec classroom, and all I can smell is something burning.

Daphne paws through the box that's cradled in Missy's hands. She shoves a neatly rolled banner and a bundle of poorly made origami flowers at me. Glitter explodes out of a bag she slaps to my chest and I sneeze. Loud.

She says, "We could do this at lunch, but I figured you'd want less of an audience."

"What are you talking about?" I think I know, but I really, really hope I'm wrong.

"So Dave heard from his cousin Marco, who works at the Donut Hut with someone who takes home ec with Si O'Mara, who says he always spends his free period making muffins." She looks at me expectantly.

"So . . . this is Si's free period?" My fingers are tight around the banner. I probably would have ripped it by now if Daphne wasn't a crazy person who had it laminated.

She nods.

Missy says, "He helps out the lesser mortals that are having trouble in class."

Which means . . . "He's not alone?" Oh god. There are going to be witnesses to this. My entire body feels like a jagged piece of ice. I'd run away, except I can't get my feet to move.

"It's not a *Prom-posal* if he's totally alone, Nolan, you need to make a statement!" Daphne throws her arms around me. "I'm so excited for you."

"Why are you ruining my life?" I say. I'm covered in purple glitter. My left eye stings and rapid blinking is only making it swell and water. I desperately don't want to know what the sign I'm holding says, and Daphne has somehow gone from hugging me to manhandling me down the rest of the hallway to the home ec room.

I can hear Missy cackling.

Struggling weakly in Daphne's hold, I ask, "How are you so strong?"

She lets me go in front of the classroom with a push to my shoulder and a bright grin.

I stand stock-still as she fusses with the banner in my hands so it's unrolled in front of me. She shoves the flowers up under my armpit—I automatically clamp down—and I somehow end up with even more glitter floating around me. I'll probably be finding it all over my body for days.

The smell of smoke and burning things is stronger here. There is no way I'm actually opening this door.

Blithely ignoring my beet red face, Daphne says, "I'll just get that for you," and twirls around me to yank it open herself.

She says, "We have to get to class, okay, but you're going to do *amazing*."

All my limbs are numb. I don't know how I actually get inside, but the door closes behind me with an ominous *thunk*.

The classroom in front of me is hazy. I'm sick to my stomach, my head feels heavy, and Si O'Mara is looking at me like I'm an alien.

Si O'Mara, angel, blessed by Ra, with eyes as blue as a dream, is staring at me. It's what I like to think of as his confused-but-curious look: a half-pout, half-smile on his mouth that he normally reserves for pop quizzes and flash fires in chemistry. He has on a soft-looking pullover, sleeves pushed up, and his blond hair is gleaming in the overhead fluorescent light.

Next to Si, *of course*, in a matching green apron, is Bern. They've got a plate of charred baked goods between them. Bern is covered in flour. I vaguely register a couple other people scattered around the room, but it's like a giant foghorn has taken out my hearing. It's possible I might pass out.

Or throw up.

Si's puzzled "What's up?" echoes bizarrely in my head.

There's an odd expression on Bern's face. I think it's *concerned*. Concerned for my mental health, probably.

Si cocks his head and says, "Is that . . . ?" and trails off, looking at the banner still clutched in my hands.

My *banner*. Asking him to prom. Holy fuck.

I say, "I'm, uh . . . ," the words rough in my throat.

Bern says, "Wow, Grant."

I widen my eyes at him desperately. Can't he just punch me in the face and put me out of my misery?

Bern's eyes narrow in response. He says, "Is that for me?"

My neck feels like a cooked noodle as I dip my head down to see GO TO PROM WITH ME? in bright green and blue puffy letters on the sign I'm clutching desperately to my chest. It . . . doesn't say *Si*, does it?

"Well . . . ," I start, uncertain of how much trouble I'd be in if I said yes. Or if I said no.

Si bounces his gaze between me and Bern like a bemused puppy.

One corner of Bern's mouth ticks up as he says, "Sure."

I blink. "What?"

"I said *sure*, Grant. Yes, I'll go to Prom with you." Bern is practically lounging back against the oven, which can't be safe. Ankles crossed, half a smirk on his face, nonchalantly holding what looks like a muffin tin full of rocks.

My "Good, great" is possibly a full octave higher than it should be.

And then I blindly stumble out of the home ec room to a blessedly empty hallway and make a beeline for the nearest bathroom.

Faint and shaky, I shove everything in a trash can by the window and lock myself in a stall. The metal of the door is gross but cooling against my forehead, and I press my hands to my ribs to keep my heart from jumping out of my chest.

My back and shoulders tense up as the bathroom door creaks open.

"Grant?"

Oh god. Oh my god, that really happened, didn't it? I accidentally asked Ira Bernstein to Prom.

"Yo, Grant," Bern says again. His boots thump hard on the floor as he walks closer.

I jump when his fist slams into the other side of the stall door, but I take a deep breath, turn the lock, and swing the door wide.

Bern has his legs apart, arms folded over his chest—the half-assed smirk has been replaced with a wide, mocking smile.

I frown at him and he shrugs.

"Don't I get a 'thanks'?" he says.

"Thanks . . . for . . ." I'm not sure what's going on here.

He rolls his eyes and drops his arms to his sides. "For saving your ass. A Prom proposal? For Si O'Mara? C'mon, Grant."

I bristle a little, because okay, maybe it was *ill-advised*, but it's not like Si would've beat me up for it or anything. I say, "It's not like—"

Only to have Bern cut me off, tugging on the ends of the banner sticking out of the trash.

"Pretty sure I saw your sister and Delgado giggling over this before school this morning. Gonna take a wild guess and say this wasn't your idea." He goes from mockingly cheerful to brooding in zero point two seconds. "Look, this doesn't have to be for real, okay? I help you out, you help me out. Right?"

I feel a little nervous, boxed in with a toilet at my back and Bern with all his broad-shouldered glory in front of me, but I don't know how to tell him to move out of my way. "Help you out . . . how?"

He shoves a hand through his dark hair, tugging on the ends lightly. "Gia and I broke up right before Prom season in the most public way possible, Grant."

Cue an awkward, lengthy pause.

Finally, I say, "So you want to, what, prove you're fine without her?" I spread my arms as far as they'll go in the narrow space. "D'you think she'd get jealous of *me*?"

Bern huffs and looks me up and down. I'd be more insulted by his expression of mild disgust if I wasn't highly aware of the fact that my sweatpants are cut off just below the knee.

Still, I press on: "Do you want her back?"

Bern sighs, stares up at the ceiling. He's got scruff along his jaw, and I watch his Adam's apple do a slow slide as he swallows. "Maybe," he says. "I don't know. Does it matter?"

It . . . actually doesn't.

"So," I say, skin itching. "Fake Prom dates. Fake dating?" *Oh my god*. "What if everyone thinks you're gay?"

"Whatever you want, Grant," Bern says. "I honestly don't give a fuck what people think about me." He grabs the front of my shirt and tugs me out of the stall. "But we should probably get out of here before lunch."

I vote for skipping lunch. I have no idea what I'm going to say to Daphne. I'm sort of numb, to be honest. I say, "Yeah, uh, why don't you go on without me?"

Bern's hand pops open over my heart, and as he releases me I glimpse a there-and-gone flash of teeth. He says, "I'm meeting up with Z, anyway. Talk to you later."

I nod dumbly, even though he's already turned away.

Five minutes later, I find myself eating lunch behind Evie's car, propped up with my back against her bumper, because she had the audacity to lock it. Numbness slowly seeps out of my limbs until my whole body is jangling with nerves.

What the fuck am I doing?

I pick apart my sandwich and ignore the buzzing of my phone in my pocket—even odds of it being Daph, wondering where I am, or Evie, wanting to know what the hell happened.

The gravelly asphalt is damp under my ass. I'm probably going to regret sitting on it when I have to get up for my next class. It smells like exhaust and wet earth in the parking lot: scents familiar and comforting. The front of a red Mazda is bumped up against my raised knees. I'm sheltered in steel and peeling paint.

Sighing, I tug out my phone—two texts from Daphne, unsurprising—and silently will time to slow down, to make my last five minutes of lunch last forever.

So, okay. All I have to do is pretend to date Bern, go to Prom with him, and keep Daphne in the dark about the fact that none of it is real.

Easy. Right.

Sure.

The rest of the day is strange.

I feel like everyone is staring at me in math class. It's possible I'm imagining things, but I swear I get more than a few smirks thrown my way, and my face heats up. I had a sparkly banner. There had been witnesses. Probably the whole school knows by now.

I manage to sneak into art class with only a low, hissed "I can't believe you," and "I have so many questions," from Evie, because bizarrely, Bern and Zamir steal Arlo's and Rob's seats across from us at our communal table in art.

Evie and I share a look. Hers full of disgruntled accusation, and mine straight-up bewildered, I'm sure.

Bern wordlessly shares my hoarded charcoals—brought

from home, because Ms. Purdy has a *budget*—and I try not to feel completely weird about it. It's not like I can say anything out loud:

What are you doing?

Stop using all my charcoals.

Are you actually trying to play foot—"Ow!"

Bern leans in across the table and says, "Try not to look like you're dying."

"You kicked me," I mutter. There'd definitely been foot nudging and then a solid, painful thump to my shin. It's going to bruise.

"You're wearing the expression of a stroke victim," Bern says. Then, through gritted teeth, "*Smile.*"

I paste on a bright, nervous grin.

Bern shakes his head. He says, "We'll work on it," and I swear the look he gives me is almost fond.

Evie scribbles *what the fuck is happening* on my sketch pad. I don't even know how to explain this to her, but I'm pretty sure she's gonna wrestle me down to the ground later and make me tell her all about it.

Six

"Okay," I say, hands up and out in surrender. I'm backed against my locker. Evie has a pointy finger digging into my sternum, and people are *definitely* staring now. "Can we talk about this later? Or somewhere more private?"

"Fine," she says, backing off a little. "You have five minutes to pack your stuff and get to my car or I will hunt you down and we'll have this conversation in front of the entire yearbook committee." She waits until I nod okay before spinning around.

I press a palm to the sore spot on my chest and watch her stalk away.

She yells, "Four minutes, twenty-nine seconds!" without looking back at me, and I scramble to get my locker open and grab all my books.

When I make it out to her car, she helps me manhandle my bike into her hatchback and waits stoically as I slide into the passenger seat and buckle in. It's breezy but sunny out, so the car is warm. She starts the car and reaches for the air conditioner, and I stare forlornly out the window; the longer she's silent, the further down in the seat I sink, shoulders up around my ears. She doesn't even have to say a word to make me feel like a kicked puppy.

I say, "I didn't do anything wrong."

I can hear her giant indrawn breath. And then: "Are you out of your mind?"

"No," I say, crossing my arms over my stomach.

"You had a banner," she says.

"Lots of people use banners," I point out, finally looking over at her. "It's not a big deal."

She waits a beat, her hesitation followed by a sigh and the thump of her fist on top of my thigh. "It's not," she says. "I know, it's just . . ." Putting the car into gear, she checks her mirror and starts reversing out of the spot. "Wanna tell me how you ended up asking Bern instead of Daphne's pre-approved choices?"

"No." I straighten up a little and roll down the window, ignoring her pointed look as she flicks off the AC. "It was an accident." *Sort of.* "We're helping each other out. He's gonna show Gia that he's over her." *Right?*

"What, over her enough to go out with a dude?" she scoffs. "And what are you getting?"

I shrug. A date? Daphne off my back? Some combination of the two, I guess. I bounce my leg a little. I keep hearing Bern's voice in my head, telling me this isn't *for real*. Just two guys, hanging out. Pretending to be close. Maybe we can be buddies afterward. At least I probably don't have to worry about him beating me up? Whatever.

Evie slants me a glance, eyes skeptical, and I shrug again.

"I don't know," I say. "I'll figure it out."

Evie drops me and my ten-speed off at the plant nursery, and I manage to hide there through dinner. Mr. Talbot orders us a pizza, clearly out of concern, since it's Friday night and I don't have a shift. Usually around now I'm getting settled down for a marathon of *Say Yes to the Dress*.

Mr. Talbot is balding, weathered, broad and thick-necked like a lumberjack, and a good two feet shorter than me.

We don't talk about our feelings and I water the houseplant section and then he firmly kicks me out the door at seven.

He says, "We're both leaving, because I have a hot date—"

I make a face.

"—and you're a teenager with, frankly, way too many plants, and you need to spend your Friday evening somewhere other than a place that *grows them*."

"You know, if I were more of a delinquent, I'd probably spray-paint a giant narwhal on the back greenhouse," I say, pouting. Probably one wearing neon sunglasses and a Guns N' Roses T-shirt.

"Please," he says, locking the main office door. "Do that. I'll even pay you."

"Wait, what?" I freeze with my ass half on and half off my bike seat.

He glances over his shoulder at me with a frown. "What, you don't think it'd look cool?"

"Uh. I don't think that's the point?"

He clasps my shoulder on his way past. "Think about it, Nolan. Now," he nudges me a little before letting go, "*go home.*"

It takes about twenty minutes to bike home, and it's full dark by the time I pull into the garage.

I hear the TV on in the den when I slip inside the house. The floorboards creak and groan as I toe off my shoes.

The water is running in the kitchen. When I peek in, Tom's at the sink washing dishes, dancing in place to, embarrassingly enough, Daft Punk. Marla's humming over her laptop at the kitchen table, and she raises one eyebrow when she catches sight of me hanging in the doorway.

She says, "I hope you ate," and, "Daphne would like to see you in the den."

"Right," I say. Right, right, right. No actual way to avoid this, then. I take a deep breath and turn around.

The den across the wide hallway has all the lights blazing, and Daphne is already peeking over the top of the overstuffed sofa with wild hair and her nighttime glasses.

"What happened?" she asks, face serious. "Nolan. What happened?"

I throw up my arms. "What *happened* is that you sent me to my doom with a sparkly banner and glitter. Bern saved me."

She clasps her hands under her chin. "Please, please tell me you're not actually dating Ira Bernstein now." She groans, presses her knuckles into her left eyebrow. "Oh my god. You're going to die."

"You told me to ask out a guy," I say, helpless.

"I told you to ask out Si!" she says, face still covered. "And now you're dating Gia Hooper's ex-boyfriend! Since when does he even like guys? Oh god, if you weren't my brother I'd just make popcorn and laugh."

I pat her awkwardly on the back. "It'll be fine."

She climbs up over the top of the couch and wraps her arms around my head like an octopus. "Shhhhh," she says, petting my hair while I struggle to breathe. "I'll protect you, don't worry. You're totally right, it'll all be fine."

———

At 10:30 A.M. on Saturday morning, I wake up and stumble downstairs to a breakfast table full of Daphne's friends and not enough waffles. Tom looks only slightly harried waving a spatula around his head, and he begs Marla to slip out to Wawa for more milk.

It doesn't work. Marla laughs and retreats to the patio with the last waffle off the iron, and Tom whips his apron over his head. "I'm going for milk. I could *not* make more waffles," he announces, hands on his hips, "but then my manhood would be in question."

"Can you get more OJ, too?" Daphne says.

Tom kisses her forehead and says, "There's more in the garage. You have legs," and then disappears out the kitchen door.

I sit down at the table and grab for some scrapple. The waffle platter in the middle of the table is distressingly empty, and Missy stares me down as she methodically cuts through her enormous three-stack.

Carlos is licking his plate clean.

Dave, in between crunches of bacon, shakes his copy of *Pride and Prejudice and Zombies* at me for no reason that I can think of, and then Carlos says, in between licking syrup off his fingers, "Gia Hooper's gonna kill you."

Daphne shushes Carlos and says, "I've got a plan: We just need to build a moat around our house and fireproof the walls."

"She's not a dragon," I say. I've heard she's frighteningly good with a blowtorch, works at her dad's garage, and straight-up punched head cheerleader Tasha Carmichael in the face at a party over the summer, but she's not an actual dragon. Probably.

"She's *dragon-like*," Daphne says. "Marco told Dave she's

a compulsive shoplifter of shiny things. She's banned from *two* malls." And then she cradles her head in her hands and says, "Oh man, the malls. I'm gonna miss having malls."

Number one: "Pretty sure State has malls, Daph."

Number two: Who actually goes to malls anymore, anyway?

Daphne's college mood swings are giving me whiplash, but at least we're veering away from the subject of Gia and Bern.

The persistent buzzing of my phone in my pocket signals a call instead of a text message, and I'm seasoned enough by now to know that I should definitely leave the room before answering it.

I don't even pull it out until I'm safely in the hallway. It's an unfamiliar number, and I answer with a wary "Hello?" when I'm halfway up the staircase.

"Grant."

"Uh." I'm 90 percent sure the guy on the other end of the line is Bern. He's got a clipped way of saying my name that always makes him seem irritated at having to talk to me. Fun. "Yeah."

There's a lengthy awkward pause, and then: "This is Bern."

I grip the railing hard, pause on the top step, and press my eyes closed. This is terrible. I say, "Hi," and marvel at how smooth I am. Wow.

Bern says, "So if we're really doing this," and stops, like

he's waiting for me to say no. A noisy breath loosens the band steadily tightening around my chest: It's a relief to find out maybe Bern thinks this is weird, too. "You should come to Mena's tonight."

Mena Dresden, hostess of infamous parties where apparently everyone gets drunk and tries not to get busted by the cops. She's got an intimidating grin and long legs and plays trumpet in jazz band.

"Tonight," I echo. "Is this a party?"

"In the sense that there will be booze, yes," Bern says.

I could say no, but then I'd probably end up being tortured by Daphne and her friends all night instead. Which is worse? It's hard to decide.

I say, "Sure. Sounds cool," and try not to take offense at Bern's snort, his "Right," and the way it floods me with an ominous sense of dread.

Bern hangs up without even saying goodbye, and I suddenly realize I'm in way over my head. I set up a research station on the patio, complete with Pop-Tarts and Tea Cooler, while Daphne and her crew start an aggressive game of croquet on the lawn.

Googling "How to fake date"—since I obviously have no idea how to *real date*, either—brings up a treasure trove of fanfiction that I bookmark for later, but is otherwise unhelpful.

Fake dating is apparently a *thing*. A trope that usually ends up with both parties having sex and living happily ever after, but that is not my life. My life is sassy cats and plants with quirky names and, before barely an hour of futile internet searching has passed, apparently a mild concussion from a croquet mallet.

"She said she was sorry!" Daphne says, holding ice up to my cheek.

Sorry for Missy is more like *sorry my blow didn't actually kill you*. "She also said I should have ducked," I say, but my head has, unsurprisingly, had worse.

I should have known better than to sit so close to them, really. Whatever Daphne and Missy play together gets hardcore and lethal fast.

Luckily, my laptop was saved from the massacre, but I bled *a lot*, and I'm worried I wasn't fast enough at minimizing my screens. Daphne seems oblivious, but Missy keeps giving me looks. It's hard to tell if they're a different sort of evil from her regular programming, though, so I just keep quiet and hope for the best.

Taking the ice from Daphne, I say, "Bern invited me to Mena's tonight."

Carefully, Daphne says, "Gia and Mena are best friends."

"Okay." Okay, so chances are good that Gia will be at Mena's, too. Awesome. This will, uh, probably play right into Bern's plans. The whole point is for Gia to see us together, right? So I just need everyone to stop looking at me like I'm three steps away from Gia disemboweling me with her claws.

Daphne strokes my temple and says, "We're gonna have to cover this up."

"I thought it'd make me look more badass."

"Oh, baby bird, no." She cups my face between her palms. "It just makes you look sad." She cocks her head. "On second thought, I think that might be better."

———

Biking to Mena Dresden's house in too-tight jeans and a T-shirt that rides up my back is uncomfortable, but not as uncomfortable as it'd be if Daphne drove me in her piece of shit car and *also* had to come back to pick me up.

The jeans and shirt are Daph's fault, obviously. I agreed to forfeit my wardrobe in exchange for being able to show up to this party alone.

She'd cried and hugged me like I was going down with the Titanic, but I'm not sure if that had to do with me, specifically, or the two hours she'd spent with Missy in the tree house out back, going through all her old Saddle Club books.

Although the porch light is on when I get there, the house is strangely quiet. There are only three cars in the driveway, and I'm not sure whether to be glad or disappointed at the general lack of noise—shouldn't there be loud music? Kids throwing up on the lawn? Multicolored flashing disco lights?

I take a deep breath and ring the doorbell before I can think too hard about it.

The door cracks open on a round of loud cheers. Mena grins at me and says, "Hey, come on in."

It's nothing like I imagined.

Mena's house has a large foyer, two staircases, a sunken living room, and not nearly as many people in it as I was expecting. Hinkey, Bennett, and Linz Garber wave at me and yell, "Grant!" as I'm shoved into the middle of a game of spoons at the kitchen table. Mena stands behind me and presses down on my shoulders. I warily take a seat.

Zamir is shuffling cards as Linz arranges all the spoons in a circle. He says, "You in?" to me, and I just nod, because why not?

Bennett and Hinkey are mixing drinks at the breakfast bar, and Bern is nowhere in sight.

It feels a little like being shoved in the deep end of the pool without knowing how to swim.

I'm almost relieved when the shouting drifts in from another room, even when I hear Gia yell, ". . . *after everything, why would you . . .*" and ". . . *ass-hat hipster wannabe . . .*" Which, for the record, I am nothing like a hipster *at all*. I have an appreciation for art that sometimes includes the absurd, but my outfits are born out of incredible laziness, not any sense of style. All my ugliness is a side effect of being too tired to care.

Linz winces, and Mena tightens her hold on my shoulders just as Gia comes sauntering in. She's got a cup dangling from her fingers, and Bern trails her into the kitchen with a dark look on his face. The sleeves of his shirt are pushed up past his elbows, and his dark brown hair is standing straight up, like he's swept his hands through it over and over again.

Gia spots me and grins, vicious at the edges. She leans over the table, and I'm only slightly surprised when her fingers slip and her plastic cup goes tumbling into my lap. Luckily, it misses my crotch, so all it does is dampen the meat of my left thigh.

"Oops." She doesn't even bother with an insincere sorry.

"Gia," Bern says tightly.

"My hand slipped." She plops down on the chair next to me and says, "Deal me in," to Zamir.

Bern looks at me, mouth pinched, and says, "Come on, Grant. Let's go."

Gia's laugh is short and unamused. "Oh no, *Nolan* wants to play, don't you?" The look she gives me is terrifying. I'm frozen to the chair, but the grip Mena has on my shoulders feels more like she's urging me up and out, now.

Bern and I have a dead-carp stare off, and Mena starts pointedly digging her thumbnails into my shoulder blades. I say, "Sure I do," and everyone else at the table groans.

"Fine," Bern says tightly. He pulls out the chair on my other side and sits down heavily. "Deal me in, too."

Spoons at home and spoons here have some very obvious differences, the biggest one being all the alcohol.

Spoons at home also involves a lot more tackling and bodily harm, though, so that's an advantage I have: I'm willing to get ruined in order to grab a spoon off the middle of the table.

Hinkey says, "It's like you're some sort of spoons *master*," although at this point the only reason I'm winning is because everyone but me is clearly shit-faced.

Gia has a mulish tilt to her jaw. I'm pretty sure me winning at spoons is making her hate me even more.

Bern, on the other hand, has gotten progressively more amused. Zamir is practically asleep at the head of the table, and Bennett's been playing the last five rounds from the floor—and losing spectacularly. By the time everyone else calls it quits, Bern's leaning back in his chair, grinning wide. He's relaxed, his whole posture welcoming. I've never seen him this open before.

Gia throws her last hand onto the table and gets shakily to her feet. She says, "Fuck you," to the whole room and Mena grabs her around the waist before she can tip over. Once Gia's relatively stable, she pushes Mena off with hushed hisses and leaves, stepping carefully as she walks toward the front door.

"You're not going to let her drive, are you?" I say, alarmed.

"With any luck she'll pass out on the front porch," Bern says. He's loose, but clearly holds his liquor better than anyone else at the table. I try not to be impressed.

Mena says, "Seriously, Ira, *really*?"

Bern rolls his eyes. He gets up, chair screeching as he pushes it back, and says, "She dumped *me*, you know," but still goes off, hopefully to see if Gia's okay.

It's a really fucking awkward situation, honestly, especially in the tense quiet after he leaves. Mena gives me a sympathetic look and sloppily pats my arm. She says, "It's just . . . they were together for a long time, you know?" like I have any investment in what is happening.

I mean, I *do*, just not in the way Mena probably thinks. Unless everyone knows this is fake except Gia. I really hope not, that would make this even weirder.

"Uh, it's okay?" I say.

Zamir starts snoring. Everyone else is zombie-staring at me—or at each other, or at the table—and this whole party is way tamer than I ever thought it would be. I figured there'd be a lot more brawls and bonfires involved. Mena lives on the edge of the state park, but so far the only one who's gone outside is her dog.

Frankly, I'm a little disappointed.

I stop myself mid-yawn, wondering if it's too early for me to just book it. Everybody looks sad and done.

"Yo, NGS." Hinkey leans across the table, reaches a bony finger toward my cheek, and says, "What the fuck happened to your face?"

I say, "Missy Delgado might be a serial killer," because

I'm pretty sure no one in this room will remember anything tomorrow anyway.

And then Linz bolts up straight in her chair and says, "I know! Let's Ouija!"

⸻

I have Daphne running interference with my curfew, but it's really not even that late when I sneak out of Mena's house. Bern never came back inside after leaving with Gia, Hinkey and Linz are arguing about the new *Witchboard* movie versus the old ones, and Mena and Bennett have gotten out all the wrong ingredients to make chocolate chip cookies.

No one will probably even notice I'm gone.

It's chilly out and Mena's house was overly warm, so I shiver on the front porch for a minute, arms crossed over my chest.

"Had enough?"

I startle at the voice, heart jumping up into my throat. Turning, I see Bern lurking against a railing in the shadows, just out of reach of the hazy, yellow-warm glow of the porch light.

"Holy shit, dude," I say. I can see the whites of his teeth as he grins at me.

"Sorry," he says, not actually sounding sorry at all.

I say, "Well, this has been, uh . . ." Not *fun*, exactly, but it was great winning at spoons for once, and I really hope Mena doesn't accidentally set her home on fire.

"Sure." He straightens up, hands in his pockets, and steps closer to me. "We should probably ramp it up a little on Monday."

I swallow hard. We're of a height, basically, except I'm a skeleton. Bern used to have a mouth full of metal and a scrappy build that blossomed into a broad-shouldered dreamboat by the start of last year. I feel like he deliberately refuses to buy jeans that actually fit his thighs. It's distracting.

"Probably," I manage. I'm not exactly sure what ramping it up is going to entail—it sounds a little scary.

Bern brushes our shoulders together softly as he walks by, back toward the front door. "Okay," he says. "See you."

There's a lingering warmth where the cotton of his long-sleeve shirt brushed my arm, and I absently rub my hand along it. "Yeah," I say faintly, but he's already back inside.

———

The house is quiet when I get in, but I'm not fooled: Daphne is around there somewhere, waiting to pounce on me like a tiger.

I almost make it to the bottom of the steps before she flies out of the kitchen and tackles me onto the floor of the den.

"How was it?" she says, hands pinning my shoulders

down. She's got her knees on either side of my waist—her hair is a halo of tangles around her head, she's got bright red lipstick on, thick black eyeliner, and a shimmer of smoky purple smeared above her eyes.

"Fine," I say. "What happened to your face?"

"I had a showdown with Missy," Daphne says. She slips off me and pushes up to her feet. Looming above me, I suddenly realize she's wearing an animal-print onesie. "Well? Did you have fun?"

I curl into a sitting position, pulling my legs up and dangling my wrists over my knees. "I think so," I say. "Maybe?"

She bends down, clasps my hands, and then tugs me to my feet. "Gia didn't maim you," she says with an *oof* when I lurch up and lose my balance into her. She pats me down briefly, starting at the top of my head. "I don't feel any open wounds."

"I'm okay," I say. "She sulked when I beat her at spoons." *Sulked* is probably the mildest word for it.

Daphne eyes me like she thinks I'm lying, but doesn't press.

I heave a sigh and let Daphne drag me across the hallway and into the kitchen, where Missy, Gator, and Dave are sitting around our kitchen table. Missy has on a plastic tiara and cat ears. There are large circles of rouge on her cheeks. Gator is wearing his shorts as a crown. Dave has on a captain's hat, with a corncob pipe sticking out of the corner of his mouth. I . . . do not actually want to know. It's like they've had the mirror opposite of my night: less alcohol and more birthday party props.

Missy smirks at me and says, "Nice pants."

They have mugs of hot chocolate, though, and a plate of Tom's snickerdoodles, so I pull up a chair.

Seven

Monday brings with it: a brand-new dick drawn on my locker, a worksheet of math SAT prep problems from Daphne—because she's *crazy*—and the start of a lawn game section in gym. You'd think that would be to my advantage, but I'm still picked last for bocce ball teams. Small Tony is pissed enough that he got stuck with me that it's nearly the end of class before I get to play.

I don't see Bern until English. Which he presumably attends just to squeeze my shoulder as he sits down. The back of my neck prickles from all the interested, prying eyes.

Evie looks at me and mouths either, *I hope you know what you're doing*, or *do I owe you watery donkey kong*, and the answer to both is a big fat no.

All I've learned so far—from my various, entirely reliable sources—is that fake dating involves a lot of hand-holding in public, hurried passionate kisses when cornered, and accidental bed sharing when there are no extra rooms at the inn.

I'm not sure about everything else, but holding hands is probably doable. I just need to make sure my palms aren't clammy and gross.

The semi-affectionate shoulder squeeze means the ball is totally in my court. When the first bell rings, I pack up my books and rub my hands on my thighs. Bern seems to be lingering, which is . . . good. He catches my gaze and jerks his head toward the door, like he's letting me know he's taking off, and I manage to slot our hands together just before he moves out of reach.

I hear Evie gasp.

Rob freezes. He looks both horrified and amused, staring at our joined hands.

Bern, for his part, only pauses a moment before tugging me closer.

He says, voice low in my ear, "I'm not really the hand-holding type," but he doesn't let me go.

I have absolutely no idea what I'm doing.

Later, I get shoved into the second-floor boys' bathroom on my way to art class. I trip through the doorway with a, "Hey," but Bern just pushes at the bag on my back until we're standing by the stall farthest from the door.

He drops his satchel on the floor and hops up onto the bank of sinks behind him like he isn't worried about his ass getting wet.

Totally confused, I ask, "What are we doing?"

He shrugs. "Skipping art." He points to the area of the floor in front of him and says, "Stand here."

"What—why?" I say, but I move toward him, hooking my fingers under the straps of my bag and hitching it up higher on my shoulders. When I'm close enough, he maneuvers me in between his spread knees, hands gripping my elbows.

He says, "There, good."

I can feel the heat of his thighs on either side of my legs. It's disconcerting, especially paired with the way he's staring at the ceiling.

"Uh," I say.

He flashes me a smirk. "Wait for it."

Wait for what, is what I want to say, but instead I shift nervously and accidentally brush up against the length of his calf. I freeze, but he doesn't react in any way other than to move forward, slipping off the edge of the sink. He catches my wrist before I can back away. I barely register the swoosh of the door opening and the faintly horrified, "*Really*, Bernstein?" Bern's eyes are deep brown, flecked with gold.

The door slamming shut makes me jump, Bern's grip loosening as I stumble backward.

Bern turns to wash his hands, avoiding my gaze when I look at him in the mirror.

I say, "What just happened?"

"Parker Montgomery the Third just caught us making out in the bathroom," he says. He flicks water at me, and then dries his hands with a paper towel.

That . . . I glance at the closed door, then back at Bern, head cocked. "Really?" I feel a little cheated. I wasn't honestly expecting desperate kisses, but like . . . we could have had desperate kisses. That was totally a situation that called for it, skipping class to hang in the bathroom, only Bern had neatly taken care of everything without any kisses at all. Huh.

And then I take in our proximity, how far apart we are now, with Bern standing by the towel dispenser near the door, as opposed to how close we were a minute ago. The deliberate touching, how Bern must have been listening for the door while I was lost in his freaking eyes. God. "You did this on purpose," I say, impressed despite myself.

He rolls his eyes. "I got caught making out with Gia *daily*, Grant," he says. "You want this to be believable, right?"

This, us, yes. Yes, I do. And it would be unfair, I think, to get my inadvisable, inexplicable, strange disappointment all over Bern. Gross.

"Thanks," I say, fiddling with the ends of my bag straps.

"Yeah, well," he says, looking anywhere but my face. "This'll get back to Gia, too."

The official reason Evie was kicked out of after-school art club our sophomore year was foul language, but it was more likely because of that time she and Arlo almost had a fist-fight about Monet. I wasn't going to stay without her, of course, and thus the Secret Awesome Sacred Art Club—or, more affectionately, SASAC—was born. We have snacks and hang out in my room Monday nights and sometimes we watch cartoons on Netflix or get smoothies from Wawa. On rare occasions, we even do art.

That afternoon, SASAC—today's medium of choice: Play-Doh—ends abruptly when Daphne comes stomping into the den just before dinner and says to me, "Into the car, baby bird, we've got places to be."

Evie gives me a look, like I've brought this on myself for my uncharacteristic and completely made-up bout of PDA, and then she flees the scene as fast as possible. She knows if she lingers too long, Daphne will just make her come, too.

I really hope Daphne doesn't want to talk about boys.

"What about dinner?" I ask. Tom's late, so he's probably bringing home burgers. Do we really want to miss that?

She shakes her purse in my face, says, "I have Goldfish. Let's go," and shoves me out the door.

I slip into the passenger seat and watch Daphne throw her arms in the air when her piece of shit car starts on the first try. She pats the dash affectionately as we back out of the driveway.

Our destination becomes apparent once we cross the

pike and turn onto the winding back roads that go through the woods. We spent the entire summer I turned fifteen here with Tom, learning to fish. Learning to fish badly and obsessively, because Daphne and Tom hate failing at anything. Marla thought it was funny. I used to chuck stones into the water and think about tagging the big rocks. And if I did more than think about it once or twice or five times, well, absolutely no one can prove it was me.

There's a looming sign that says the reservoir is closed, but the gates are still swung wide open.

The lot is mostly empty. There's a dark SUV on one end, next to an old overturned canoe crawling with moss, and two cars parked next to each other close to the paths that lead down to the water. A lean and rangy fox darts across the gravel and disappears into the trees as we turn in.

Daphne parks sideways, takes up three spaces, and then slips out and clambers up onto the roof.

I eye her from the ground on the passenger side, but she makes impatient hand motions until I pull myself up to join her. The steel frame groans under our combined weight, listing slightly to the left, like half the tires are deflated. It's an aging rust bucket of death. I really hope the roof doesn't cave in.

The water, peeking out from between the trees, is reflecting the hot orange of the sky, shimmering like fire even though it's still a few hours from sunset.

Daphne says, "Look, Nolan," and places a hand on my raised knee. "Everything the light touches is our kingdom."

I groan and say, "Oh no," barely resisting a face-palm. I mean, at least this probably isn't about Bern. That's sort of a plus.

She ignores me and says, "A king's time as ruler rises and falls like the sun. One day, Nolan, the sun will set—"

"Are you seriously giving me the *Lion King* speech?" I cut in. "You realize this is the exact same speech your dad gave to me when I was first adopted, right?"

"I'm trying to give you my car, asshole," she says, exasperated.

"You can't give me your car." I knock on the roof underneath us and wince at an ominous creak.

She punches me in the arm. "I'm giving you my car to *use*, okay? Don't be a douchebag. I can't take it to college, and I'm not letting you bike it in the snow next year, or," she shudders dramatically, "take the bus."

The bus is a cesspool of vomit and noogies and freshmen. I will happily not take the bus until the end of my days.

"Thank you," I say, trying for the proper amount of sincerity.

She leans into my side, head on my shoulder. "You're very welcome," she says. And then, "Oh, Roxanne, you magnificent beast, what am I going to do without you?" She gives the car a fond pat.

"Probably live longer," I say, and then laugh when she

tackles me into rolling all the way down the back onto the trunk. I grip the radio antenna like a lifeline, and it breaks off in my fist as I slide down over the bumper and hit the ground. "Oops?"

Daphne is sprawled out on her stomach across the back window. She props her chin up in her hands and looks down at me and says, "Let's go drop Goldfish in the shallows and see what we can catch."

Nothing. The answer is absolutely nothing—we can't even catch anything with worms—but I stand up and shrug. "Okay."

We drive back in full dark, windows rolled down to let in the cool night air. Daphne's face is strangely set, mouth a pensive line. The streetlights make her skin glow, and she flicks me a look when I nudge her side.

"What?" she says.

I shrug. "You okay?"

Her hands flex on the steering wheel. She says, "Sure."

Daph and I don't really talk about feelings. We share silent, mutual hugs when we're sad, hand-holding in the dark on sleepless nights, sniffles buried in poignant episodes of *Supernatural* or *Brooklyn Nine-Nine*.

I know she liked Adrian a lot, despite all his monstrous asshole tendencies. She'd been deaf to everyone's warnings, most likely because of his fine man-abs and the way his smile sparkled in the sun. I'm not going to say "I told you so," though, because that would be ungentlemanly and also probably make her feel even more like crap.

Instead, I drape my hand over the console in between us, palm up, and say, "Hey."

She side-eyes me but relaxes her death grip on the wheel. Her hand drops gracelessly over mine, like a deliberate accident.

Palm to palm, I squeeze our fingers together and hold on.

Eight

At school, dating Bern apparently gives me some notoriety. People who didn't even know I was alive are looking at me in new and disturbing ways. In the halls, in classes, at lunch. It's been less than a week, and I've gotten more nods and waves and glares than my entire past three years here. It's making me tense.

"That's weird, right?" I ask Evie after a lacrosse sopho-more lifts his upper lip in a wordless snarl when we pass by his locker in the morning.

I've never been anyone's favorite, but the blatant ani-mosity some people are sending me is giving me hives.

Later, on my way to lunch, I notice Si. It's hard *not* to notice Si, an Apollo in a soft-looking cream sweater with thumbholes, dark pants tight across his thighs. The hallway lights make his hair look like spun gold. Also: He's smiling right at me. For real this time. I think.

Somehow, I manage to not walk into a wall. "Uh, hi?"

"Nolan, right?" he says. Two of his bottom teeth are slightly crooked; it just makes the rest of him look even more perfect. "We have science together."

We've had science together every semester for three years, but okay.

I say, "Sure," because there is something wrong with my brain.

Si grins wider. He nods and says, "The GSA meets after school on Thursdays," which is . . . what? I feel like he's in the middle of a conversation that we weren't actually having.

He's looking at me expectantly, though, and I say, "Yeah?"

"You should come," Si says, and I choke down a hysterical laugh and my instinctive *no*.

Daphne would love this. This whatever the hell is happening right here. Si looks earnest, and I'm super confused. "Uh."

"Bring Bernstein," Si says, shoving his hands in his pockets. "We'd love to have both of you."

There is absolutely no way I'm going to be able to get Bern to go to GSA with me. That's just—I shake my head—*no*.

Si looks ridiculously crestfallen at that, and somehow his dismayed expression makes him look *even more hot*. Jesus. It's just unfair. Heartbreaking. It makes my hands feel empty, like I should be curving them over his shoulders and letting him cry into my collarbone.

I manage to say, "I'll think about it?"

The power of Si's answering grin slices through the midday gloom of the hallway. It's like—this guy is great at everything. Football, being gay, smiling. He's aced being alive, and he's only seventeen. There are very specific ways I wish he would use that with me.

"Great," Si says, clapping me on the shoulder so hard I stumble. "Great. *Awesome.* Hope to see you there."

I'm not actually sure how I get to the caf. I'm just there, suddenly, still mostly thinking *What the fuck just happened?*

Daphne watches me like a hawk as I sit down and take out my lunch, fingers tapping uneven beats on the table. Apple, sandwich, cookies, Yoo-hoo. A napkin, a little note from Tom that says *Go get 'em, tiger*, a plastic bag of Cheerios that I'd hastily stuffed in for breakfast and then completely forgotten about.

Finally, she cups her chin in her hands, elbows on the table, and sinks down low in her seat. "So," she says, drawn out nice and slow, "what were you talking to Si about?"

Very carefully, I say, "Nothing."

Carlos snorts into my packet of Oreos, and I make a face at him.

"Really," Daphne says, grinning, "because I could have *sworn*—"

"No," I say, pointing a finger first at her, and then at Dave, who's been ignoring us in favor of reading *The Glass*

Bead Game, but is fooling absolutely no one. Dave is just as nosy as Daphne.

She rolls her eyes. "It wouldn't kill you to join a club that fosters understanding and friendship!"

"I said I'd think about it," I shoot back, mistakenly thinking she'll drop the subject. Daphne has never dropped any subject ever.

"Look," she says. "I think you should have some friends that aren't us and art weirdos." She looks perfectly serious, but her own friends are either robot demons or Carlos—I don't see how she can talk to me about this.

"Why? How is this an actual problem?" I ask.

"Because we're all graduating, Nolan," Daph says, nodding sagely, "and then you'll be a pathetic party of two." She holds up her fingers, "You and Evie. On good days you could *maybe* count Arlo Mahmoud and Rob Richards, if you can convince Rob that Evie won't eat him."

There's absolutely nothing wrong with any of that.

Daphne shrugs. "I just think you should try. Safe-sex pamphlets, bake sales, plants. You love plants! The GSA is in charge of After Prom, too. Banners and decorations: You can show how much you rock at that stuff."

I know she's trying to be encouraging, but it sounds terrible.

Carlos crunches through a Cool Ranch Dorito and says, "Dude, maybe those lacrosse douchebags'll stop throwing balls at your head in gym."

It's a good argument. I cover my face with my hands and groan. Daphne pats the top of my head. I haven't totally given in yet, but she probably senses it's only a matter of time.

———

Bern is slouching against my locker after school. I'm surprised to see him there, mainly because I didn't think he had any idea where my locker actually was.

He nods at me and then says, "We should hang out before Art Buddies."

"Okay," I say, slightly dubious. I wonder if *hanging out* means loitering in front of the Wawa, or out behind the auditorium, or if I'm finally going to see the woods by Mena's house.

It takes me three embarrassing tries to unlock my locker, and when it finally clicks, it refuses to actually open. I jiggle it, can feel it catch on something—my hoodie, maybe, or the plastic bag I had my gym uniform in—and only jump a little when Bern slams his fist into it with a sigh. The locker opens with a shaky clang, and I do not find his pleased smirk at all stupidly endearing.

"Thanks," I say, grabbing my history and math books and shoving them into my backpack.

He shrugs instead of answering. It reminds me that I

know absolutely zero about this guy. Or that I know stupid shit, rumors, and that he was in love with Metal Shop Gia.

Evie, at her own locker halfway down the hall, makes an exaggerated baffled face at me behind Bern's back. She jerks her head toward the stairs and I frown.

Bern follows my gaze and seems to slouch even further into the wall. He says, looking from me to Evie, "Unless you have plans," like there hasn't been at least five minutes of almost complete silence between us.

I feel weird. And achy. And my shoulder blades are sweating.

I take a deep breath and say, "No. It's fine."

———

I never gave much thought to how Bern got around before. Whether he has a car, or whether one of his friends drives him places, or whether he has anything other than the motorcycle I've seen him on, usually with Gia and her own bike out in front. I should have, though, seeing as how I'm now staring at his beat-up monstrosity idling by the curb, a spare helmet clutched in my hands.

"Uh," I say.

He's already swung astride and revved up the engine, long legs replacing the kickstand. He stares over at me expectantly.

"Uh," I say again. I spare a longing glance at my lone ten-speeder on the bike rack.

"I'll drive you back here after," Bern says. "C'mon."

That's not actually my concern. My problem is that Bern wants me to ride on something that's possibly even more of a deathtrap than Daphne's car. I'm hoping my face isn't giving away my complete horror.

I think motorcycles are rad *in theory*, but in reality should only be used for road trip movies and gay porn. Or by people who are not me.

"Grant," Bern says impatiently.

I sigh and shove the helmet on my head. I say, "You should probably call me *Nolan*, you know." Gingerly, I swing onto the back of the bike. My hands clench and unclench on nothing and air before I grab onto the sides of Bern's jacket.

Over his shoulder, he says, "You're gonna have to hold on tighter than that," with a sharp slice of a grin, and then he takes off.

I end up clutching Bern around the waist, ducked down against his back with my eyes firmly closed. If I concentrate on the heat of his body all up and down my front, cradled in my legs, then I don't have to think about how we could die on a tight turn, and how my hair is probably going to be a sweaty mess with a rat's nest on the end, given the way it's whipping in the wind below the helmet.

I don't even notice we've gotten anywhere until he cuts

the engine, and then it takes a few wobbly steps on the side-walk before I realize we're in front of Ground Zero. Huh.

"How did you . . . ?" I start.

He rolls his eyes, hooks his helmet on the back of the bike, and says, "I pay attention, *Nolan*."

My cheeks heat and I busy myself with unstrapping my helmet and trying to run my fingers through my hair. They get stuck and I wrinkle my nose.

Bern nudges me and says, "The trials of having aging–rock star hair," before moving past me and slinking inside. Who moves like that at seventeen? Like an eel or a snake or a cheetah, when I haven't even fully grown into my puppy paws yet and have the talent of being able to trip over thin air. Truly, it's unfair.

It's crowded enough that Tamara only has time to waggle an eyebrow at me as she rings up our orders, but she says, "Evie will have questions," when she hands over our change. I'm actually surprised Evie isn't here already. And a little relieved.

I hitch a shoulder at Bern as we walk away and say, "That's Evie's girlfriend."

The way Bern says, "Sure," makes me think maybe he already knew.

Huh.

My regular table is empty and waiting for me and Evie, so I lead Bern there and hope Evie forgives me for it. The wall next to it still has a doodle of Peekaboo in a necktie from the day before. His beady little eyes are judging me. It'd probably look strange if I flipped him off. The dog, not Bern.

Nervously, I rub my palms on my thighs as I sit down.

Bern slouches low in the seat across from me, the drink he ordered slowly sweating a ring around the napkin under it.

"So," I say, hands around my own cup of hot chocolate, "we should, uh, get to know each other?" That's something that people do on dates, right? Oh god, this is a date. I mean, it's *not* a date, but it's also definitely supposed to be date-*like*.

Bern spreads his hands. "I know a lot about you," he says.

"You do." It's not really a question, even though I'm not sure I actually believe him. What could he know about me? That I suck at gym? Pretty sure the entire school knows that by now, even the ones who have no idea who I am.

He straightens up in his chair, leans forward with his elbows on the table. "Nolan Grant no-hyphen Sheffield, summer baby, has a hard-on for narwhals, attached at the hip to Evie Cho, sucks at drawing faces, wants Purdy to drop dead." He quirks an eyebrow at me, one corner of his mouth up in something like amusement. "Did I miss anything?"

A lot, I want to say, like how I only suck at faces because Ms. Purdy is an asshole, that I got caught vandalizing public property by the cops on three separate occasions before I was ten, that I watch *Tiny House Nation* on demand and will eat basically anything except roast beef. I open and close my mouth a couple times and then say, "I like plants."

Bern . . . cracks up.

He goddamn *giggles*, burying his face in his hands. I have to save his soda from getting shoved off the table.

"Okay," Bern says, laughter petering off. His eyes are bright and his cheeks are red and he's grinning at me when his hands fall away. "Okay, so, *plants*, huh?"

"We should talk about you," I say hastily.

He still looks way too amused, but he says, "I'm game."

Over the course of an hour I learn:

Bern is definitely failing English. But Mrs. Rahm is giving him enough extra credit for helping out with the chess team that he'll probably pass anyway. He seems mostly okay with this, even though his shoulders tense up when he admits it. My gut feeling is that it's grossly unfair? I would rather play chess than read *Pygmalion*, but then again, I have no idea how to play chess. Bern must be really good at it.

And although his friends Hinkey and Bennett have after-school detention straight through until the end of the year, he smirks at me and says, "Me and Zamir have never officially been caught." Which is fucking *ridiculous*.

He shrugs and says, "We don't rat each other out. No one knows for sure I was behind paintballing the basketball team."

"*Everyone* knows that," I say, but I guess his point is that no one can actually prove it.

Bern says, "They deserved it. For Benny," and I vaguely remember Bennett embarrassing himself at tryouts last year—maybe it wasn't so much Bennett embarrassing himself as the basketball team being douchewads.

Also:

Bern has a tattoo. A couple. I knew this, objectively, but I didn't actually *know this*, and I have to curl my fingers into my palm to keep from touching when he rolls his sleeve all the way up. I can just about see the ends of a thick purple tentacle curling over his bicep. It should be terrible. It should be gnarly, sea-captain tacky. The shading is perfect, though, the delicate sucker cups realistically fantastic.

"How did that happen?" I ask, fascinated.

He smooths his sleeve back down and says, "Ink and needles, Grant."

"Funny," I say.

His eyes are smiling when he says, "Z sketched it out, but my tattoo guy did a really good job."

He has a tattoo guy. That somehow doesn't even make him sound like a dumbass.

Our knees knock under the small table. I tug my legs back, but we're both too tall to fit, really. I've got the leg-span of a praying mantis, and I end up feeling the warmth of his thighs bracketing one of mine.

I clear my throat, heat crawling up my spine, and fiddle with Bern's straw wrapper. I say, "Can you believe Daphne's making me do SAP?"

Considering why and what Bern and I are currently doing with each other, he probably can.

But apparently Bern's some kind of math supergenius, and the last twenty minutes before Art Buddies is dedicated to him filling out my SAT-prep sheet for that day. It's amazing. I usually get them all wrong. Daphne's going to be suspicious as hell, but it's worth it.

———

I can feel Evie's eyes on me when Bern and I walk into Art Buddies. When I glance over at her, though, she just scratches her cheek with her middle finger, the corner of her mouth curling up. I bark a short laugh, twist my ratty hair up into a bun, and shove a paintbrush through it.

Bern reaches out to ruffle Mim's hair on his way past to his own station. She ducks away and glares at him.

And then she takes all her wrath out on me by deciding to finger paint. Those are a bitch to wash off, and Daphne made me wear my tight jeans today. On second thought, this is a pretty good idea. I could use an excuse to never have to wear these again.

After an hour that goes by surprisingly quickly, Evie comes up behind me, says, "I'm taking you home," and levels Bern a glare that dares him to contradict her.

He shrugs, says, "Later, Grant," and . . . squeezes the back of my neck. My *nape*. Calloused fingers held there for a one-two-three beat that makes my chest flush. I didn't know fake dating would involve so much touching. I don't exactly mind, but Evie's eyeing me up like I'm only two steps away from having a mental breakdown.

In the car, I say, "Tamara told you all about it already."

"Tam told me you spent an hour talking with a, quote, *handsome loner-type with over-styled hair and a goofy laugh,*" Evie says, shooting me a look. "She said you let him do your homework."

"Daphne's crazy SAT-prep worksheet doesn't count as homework." I wisely leave the comment about his laugh and hair alone.

"You rode on his motorcycle," she says.

Well. "You saw me leave school with him. I wore a helmet!" My hair still hasn't recovered. I stole the paint-brush from Art Buddies so Daphne wouldn't see.

Her hands flex on the steering wheel, mouth pressed closed. It's uncomfortably silent for the ten or so minutes it takes to get back to the high school and shove my bike into her trunk.

Finally, she says, "I'm just worried about you."

"The motorcycle wasn't that bad." I feared for my life, yeah, and it tended to go faster than I feel anything without a steel shell around me should go on a road with other, big-ger metal things that could crush both it and me, but . . . "I'm hoping he won't make me do that again."

She makes a disbelieving noise. "Yeah, *okay*."

I flick the side of her head and she slaps my hand away.

"Oh my god, Nolan," Daphne says as soon as I get home, dragging me into the den.

My nose itches, I can feel paint drying on my forehead, and there's a solid chance my pants are ruined, which is the only mildly okay thing to come out of that afternoon. I want to get changed and eat three helpings of whatever smells so delicious in the kitchen.

"Oh my god." Her eyes are enormous and her hands are shaking.

"What happened?" I ask, suddenly worried.

She reaches up and grabs my ears and drags my face down close to hers. She says, "You made out with Bern."

"Uh." Old news, right? I guess the only reason I was blessedly free of Daphne-teasing for that is because she didn't actually know about it until now. And I can't even deny it. "I did."

"How was it? Did you use tongue? No," she makes a face, "don't answer that. Gross, ugh." She lets me go, throwing her arms up in the air. "I can't believe you didn't tell me! First kisses!" Narrowing her eyes, she says, "It was your first kiss, right?"

"Yes?" I say, feeling like shit for lying to her. Like, it's terrible, and then on top of that I didn't even get to kiss anyone. I'm still kiss-less. The only scandalous things I've done are hold hands and use the same straw when Bern let me finish up the last of his soda. I guess I can still get mono. "It was good." Good's good. Not too bold a statement, better than fine.

"Good," she echoes. "Good is for pizza, baby bird. Good is for an enjoyable movie, or a game of Risk—"

Nobody thinks a game of Risk is good, especially not one played by the Sheffield family.

"—good isn't for first kisses!"

I don't know, maybe I'd think it was a bigger deal if it was actually a thing that happened.

She shoves both hands into her hair, fluffs it out crazily, and says, "How did this happen? Why wasn't I immediately informed?"

"Daphne," I say. "Bern and I are dating." I'm not an expert, but I'm pretty sure people who date are expected to kiss. This isn't shocking news.

"I just thought—" Daph stops, looks hard at me. "You really like Bern? For real?"

I feel like I've swallowed a handful of bees, throat sore and chest buzzing. "Yeah," I say, and it doesn't even sound like a lie.

Nine

There is one main reason I ultimately decide to go to the GSA meeting on Thursday, and that's because Si sends me what can only be described as a hopeful look during chemistry, and I'm weak.

I almost chicken out anyway, though.

For one, Evie refuses to go with me:

"My rune will catch fire and my hair will go up in flames," she says dispassionately, clanging her locker shut. She looks up at me, face blank. "If you wanna go, that's your funeral."

"Um." I half thought she'd plead with me not to go, or drag me bodily from the building. I feel sad and abandoned now.

And then she grabs a shank of my hair and tugs my face down close to hers—"Ow, fuck, *Evie*"—and says, "Text me immediately after or I'll kill you."

For two, Bern is waiting at my locker again.

I say, "I—*we've* been . . . invited to check out the GSA?" when he asks me what I'm doing before Art Buddies.

He laughs like I'm joking, but not, like, the helpless, goofy laughter from Tuesday. More like I've said something really dumb.

I frown and say, "It's not a bad idea."

"It's a terrible idea, Grant," Bern says, laughter paused to look at me like I'm crazy. "The lacrosse team wants to grind you into blood and bones."

I cross my arms over my chest, frowning. "Yeah, but not because I'm *gay*."

His expression turns momentarily bewildered. "Does that actually make a difference? Si O'Mara's—"

"Nice?" I cut him off. I don't really want to hear his honest opinion about Si. Si is, from most sources, amazing. "A stand-up guy?"

He mouths *a stand-up guy* back at me, hands deep in his pockets. He bobs his head, though, saying, "Okay. Okay, Grant. You do what you gotta do. I'll see you later."

For some reason it makes the back of my eyeballs burn. Fuck.

So what I really want to do, what would be awesome, is to go home and crawl under my covers and watch *Unbreakable Kimmy Schmidt* on my laptop until Daphne finds me.

Instead, I take a deep, fortifying breath and make my way down to the GSA room.

By day, the GSA meeting room is the home ec classroom. The scene of my *Prom-posal*. Ugh. I couldn't really drink in the atmosphere then, though, considering my nerves and tunnel vision, but now I see: the line of sewing machines under the bank of windows, the three unwieldy stoves, the five microwaves that look seriously gross. There are clear bins of what look like ribbons, buttons, and fabric scraps scattered everywhere, and a U-shape of chairs around a green shag area rug.

Si waves at me with a potholder, a sheet of cookies in his other hand. They smell like cinnamon and heaven.

I stick my hands in my pockets and slouch against the back wall.

There are clumps of kids standing around talking: at least half the lacrosse team, including the ever-delightful Small Tony; Tasha Carmichael and a handful of cheerleaders; Mykos; Padme, our lone girl football player; Parker Montgomery the Third; and two dudes I don't recognize. There are also a couple of giddy-looking probably-freshmen with hearts in their eyes as they snag cookies from Si when he starts carrying around a plate of them.

It's sickening.

Si stops in front of me with a smiling, "Cookie? They're cinnamon oatmeal–chocolate chip," and when I bite into one it feels like I'm eating a little piece of his soul. They're, outrageously, better than anything Tom has ever baked, and everything Tom makes is fantastic. Screw heart-eyes, I'm pretty sure I'm drooling. It'd be embarrassing if anyone but Si even noticed I was in the room.

His smile morphs into a full-grown grin. He says, "Good, huh? It's my nana's recipe."

There are no words for how perfect Si O'Mara is. The surprising thing would be if I *didn't* have a giant crush on him.

The dry erase board at the front of the room has three things listed on it in alternating colors: *After Prom!!!* (three exclamation points, someone's excited), *Plant sale*, and *Get art guy to help with posters/decorations*. I guess I'm art guy. I'm not surprised at all that they couldn't remember my name.

Si places the now half-full plate on a desk and claps his hands to get everyone's attention. He says, "Okay, guys, let's talk After Prom!"

What follows is an hour of brainstorming decoration themes, followed by a solidification of plant sale plans to fund After Prom—during which I press my mouth closed to keep from blurting out things about succulents—and then finally someone says, ". . . art guy," and my head snaps up from where I've been idly penning black flowers all over my beat Converse sneakers.

Everyone is staring at me.

I'm suddenly extremely conscious of my ink-stained fingers, all the holes in my pants, and the giant T. rex sticker I slapped on my chest that morning to cover an OJ stain.

"Um," I say. "What?"

Si says, like an overly eager puppy, "You're friends with Zamir Abadi, right?"

I'm pretty much not friends with Zamir at all. But Tasha Carmichael has her mouth pursed expectantly, and a couple lacrosse assholes are snickering. I sink down lower into my seat and say, "He's friends with Bern. Why?"

"We were hoping you could—" Si pauses, staring at me.

I'm not sure what's showing on my face, but it might be intense disgust. I'm not even "art guy." Art guy has a name. I'm just a random slob at the back of the room. Christ. No wonder Si told me to bring Bern.

"You know what?" Si says, smile barely faltering. "Never mind. *You're* in art, right? Do you want to help with the posters?"

The only thing worse than thinking I was art guy is actually just being *substitute* art guy. But what am I going to do, say no? Small Tony's probably just itching for a reason to throw even more balls at my head in gym.

I cross my arms over my chest and say, "Okay," and, "But you guys might want to rethink your plant sale strategy," while I've got the room.

———

I'm not too surprised to find Evie holding my bike captive after the GSA meeting lets out. After I texted her *still alive* as soon as I slipped out the door.

"Have you been here the whole time?" I ask. She should have just come with me. That way she could have saved me from volunteering to help coordinate decorations for After Prom. I don't know what I'm doing, but Si's grin can be very persuasive.

She says, "This was taped to your bike," and shakes a piece of paper in my face. "Do you think it's from Gia?"

I grab at it and see . . . a pretty decent stick figure hangman. There's a menacing, handwritten (x—x) emoticon that I'm almost entirely certain means I'm dead.

"I can handle it," I say. I don't really get Gia's deal, if it is from her.

"She probably thinks you're taking advantage of Bern's broken heart," Evie says, crumpling up the note and tossing it in the trash can at the bottom of the stairs. "This better not get you killed. Over *nothing*."

I pitch my voice comically high and say, "Hey, Nolan, how was your totally awesome and not tragic at all foray into the GSA? Tell me all about it!"

"Who says *foray*, you nerd?" Evie says, shoving at my shoulder.

I start walking my bike to her car. "Apparently I'm now in a month-long committed relationship with an Under the Sea–themed After Prom party."

"You didn't," she says, stopping in the middle of the parking lot.

The front of my tire bumps up against her calf. "I can't be responsible for my sans-Evie actions. If you didn't want me to volunteer for stupid shit, you shouldn't have left me alone with Si."

She groans. "Tell me you're not in charge of decorations."

A month ago, the biggest social event of my week was our Secret Awesome Sacred Art Club. I spent the rest of my time divided between school, eating Tom's food, napping in front of the TV under piles of afghans with Daphne, and listening to Rilo Kiley's *Execution of All Things* album on repeat, locked in my room with Fuzzbutt.

I don't know if this current change is for the better.

"I could," I say, "but that would be a big fat lie."

———

I muddle through Art Buddies with both Mim and Bern being in a *mood*. I'm not fully equipped to deal with either of them like that, so I'm exhausted by the time I get home.

After dinner, lying on my back in the middle of my bed, Fuzzbutt a heavy, furry lump on my chest, I rub my thumbs into his ears and listen to him purr.

I can hear Daphne and Tom shouting *Jeopardy!* answers at the TV downstairs.

Marla knocks on the frame of my door, then peeks in

with a smile and a slice of pie. "You didn't eat your dessert." Marla is small like a sprite, whip-lean, with a blotchy pink birthmark on the inside of her left arm. Daphne got Marla's hair, her wide smile, and her large brain—she got Tom's freckles and athletic shoulders and his completely insane idea of what constitutes fair play. Although that last one may have come from both sides of the family, given Marla's tendency to bend the rules at Scrabble.

When I don't move, she says, "Trying to decide whether it's worth it to kick Fuzzy off?" Lifting the plate higher she lilts, "It's a la mode."

I wrinkle my nose and heave up into a sitting position. Fuzzbutt digs his claws into my chest and then rolls down unhappily into my lap before using my groin as a springboard.

Marla sits down on the edge of my bed and hands me the plate. She waits until I take a giant gooey bite of apples before saying, "So you're dating a boy."

I very carefully don't choke on my mouthful.

"Is he nice?" she asks.

I swallow thickly. "Do we have to talk about this?"

"Well"—she spreads her hands—"I didn't ask Daphne about Adrian, and we all know how that turned out."

We know, because Adrian Fells is definitely not nice.

"Bern is . . ." I trail off. Is Bern nice? I'm not actually sure. "Okay. He's fine. He's helping me with all the math work Daphne's shoving at me."

"He drives a motorcycle," Marla says. "Daphne says his ex-girlfriend has access to sharp tools."

"I'm careful," I say. "And I wear a helmet."

She tilts her head, unimpressed, probably because she knows I stash my Ninja Turtles helmet behind the Carsons' bushes when I bike to school in the mornings. I'm not always great at remembering to put it back on before getting home.

"I *do*," I say. I don't admit to having her same reservations about Bern's two-wheeled monster, that's just like dumping blood in the water.

"Right." She pats my leg and stands up. "Just so you're being careful. About *everything*. It's fine to explore yourself—"

I gag a little.

Marla goes on like I'm not steadily turning green. "Nolan, you're a young man now—"

"Oh, dear lord," I say without actually meaning to. This is starting to sound like the beginning of her sex talk. Daphne and I had gripped hands through that horrific adventure nearly two years ago. It was unneeded then, and it is definitely unneeded now.

"Look, this is nothing to be embarrassed about," she says, but she seems to give up, shoulders slumping slightly. I feel bad about it for zero point two seconds, and then I remember she'd used puppets to *illustrate*. "I'm trying to be supportive."

"I'm fine," I say. "I know what I'm doing." I have no idea what I'm doing, but Marla doesn't need to know that.

"I'm sure you do," Marla says. Her clear confidence in me only makes me feel a little bad for lying. "But your father and I are always here if you need to talk."

Ten

Most Saturdays I have a long shift at the Talbot plant nursery, which is occasionally broken up by Evie bringing me lunch.

It's probably my imagination, but all the plants seem to curl away from Evie when she stalks through the rows toward me. She's holding a brown paper bag, and it swings dangerously close to the pots as she moves.

She's wearing way too much black for the heat of the day, but she offsets it with a frilly-edged pink parasol shading her head from the high noon sun.

She says, "So there's a rumor going around that Si O'Mara's into you, but there's an eighty-twenty chance Gia Hooper started it."

I let out a deep breath. "So it could be bunk."

"It's most definitely bunk," she says, sweeping past me and leading the way to the picnic tables around back.

"Hey." She doesn't need to sound *that* sure of it. I mean, there are low odds that I'm suddenly attracting someone who never even knew I existed before last week, but still.

I rush to right a flat of pansies that tips precariously toward the ground as she walks by. My foot kicks out to push a display pot of ferns back onto a low shelf on the other side of the row.

She glances over her shoulder at me. "Really?"

I scowl down at the scarred wood as she sets out our lunch—sodas, sandwiches from Ground Zero, a bag of chips, and two brownies. "I'm a catch," I say.

"A catch of what," she says. "That's the question." She has a grin winking at the corner of her mouth.

I flick a chip at her, and say, "Jerk."

She flicks a chip right back at me and looks over my shoulder. "Oh my god, what the hell, here comes—"

"Hey! Nolan!"

"Oh, uh." I twist in my seat and glance up at Si. "Hi." There's a slight breeze ruffling the ends of his fine blond hair. The sky blue cotton T-shirt stretching over his chest matches the shade of his eyes. He grins down at me and my heart turns over. Yep, all that is still doing it for me. Awesome.

My fingers feel thick and heavy, and the soda can gives a metallic crinkle when they flex around it.

No amount of sun can possibly hide my blush.

And then Evie kicks at my feet and says, "O'Mara," and I realize we've just been staring at each other like silent creeps.

He clears his throat. "So I figured maybe you could help me make a list of plants for our sale?"

"How did you know I was working today?" I say, swinging my legs over the bench and standing up.

Across the table, Evie alternately widens and narrows her eyes in a way that means absolutely nothing to me. Is she having some sort of an attack?

"I . . . didn't?" Si says.

I don't know if that means he was just wandering around, hoping I'd be here, or if he just figured it didn't actually matter if I was or not. Technically, anyone here could help him. I'd already told them my two cents about succulents at the meeting.

He looks sheepish, though, at a quick glance.

I stare down at my hands, hyperaware of the dirt ground into my fingernails.

"So, uh," I say, hunching my shoulders. "Little pots and mini-gardens will probably sell pretty well." I know Mr. Talbot's involved with the plant sale every year, but he's probably not going to be super happy that I talked the GSA out of helping him clear out his leftover Easter and spring inventory. "I can show you around our houseplant greenhouse?"

Si nods. He says, "I really appreciate this." He cups a hand around my elbow, and my skin tingles where his fingers slide under the hem of my T-shirt.

I don't exactly go breathless, but it's harder than usual to manage actual words. My "No problem" goes embarrassingly quiet on the tail end, like my voice gives out.

I can practically hear Evie wince behind me.

It doesn't seem like Si notices, though. He just changes his grip as I step past him, moving his hand down to shackle my wrist loosely, almost like we're holding hands. His grin widens. He says, "C'mon then," and tugs on my arm.

I shoot a bewildered, half-panicked look at Evie over my shoulder. She looks just as confused as me, mimes twisting my arm out of Si's grip, but do I *really* want to do that?

That might be rude.

There's an exciting thrum to my heart, like butterfly wings fluttering inside my chest. My brain feels nervous-happy. Something in my throat wants me to straighten up and howl. It's not like I haven't gotten weird boners in the greenhouses before, but usually I'm all alone. So the wise course here, *probably*, would definitely be to shake Si loose. Right.

But then Si drops my hand to drape an arm across my shoulders and all my limbs jerk forward like they're on puppet strings.

I stumble just enough to glance my hip off a fence post.

My face is flaming. I clear my throat—can I be any more of a spaz?—and say, "Uh, right this way."

Si is gracious. Si is funny in a way that shouldn't be funny, like when he wiggles his eyebrows over the pussy willow. Si's so sweet it makes my teeth ache, particularly when he coos over the resident baby wild bunnies that nested under our row of annuals. Si is any number of adjectives that can also be applied to Daphne's eighty-year-old Gram, so it's crazy that all of that adds up to godlike hotness.

"He's got the personality of a wet noodle," Evie says when Si finally leaves. She holds up my phone, which I'd left on the picnic table. "Also, Bern invited you to Mena's tonight."

Another exciting evening of drunken spoons and getting threatened by Gia. Awesome.

"I told him you were bringing me, too," she says.

"Hold on to your hat for a wild and crazy ride," I say drily. If she's lucky, we'll even try to contact the dead again.

She gathers up her trash and my mostly uneaten lunch and chucks it into the can. Bees are already starting to gather, the heat of the midday sun drawing them out. I can't wait for full summer.

"Do you think you can make it out of the house without Daphne knowing?"

I shrug. "A boy can dream."

———

It's not that I don't want Daphne to know where I'm going, it's that I don't want her to dress me up. She keeps getting onto kicks where she makes me wear tight clothes and jeans that are too short, like my knobby ankles are so appealing. They're pale as pure bone and just make my feet look even bigger.

"You look like you're going to a sock hop," Evie says when I duck into her car.

My phone buzzes with a text and I have to wriggle around to get it out of the obscenely tight front pocket of my pants. Two successive texts from Bern are on the screen. Both say, *Are you here.*

"Am I there?" I say absently. How can he not know that I'm not there yet? Mena's house isn't that big, I don't think I could get lost in it.

And then ten minutes later Evie turns onto Mena's street and says, "Whoa."

This is not a drunken spoons party.

There are people all over the lawn. It looks like some-one's puking in a rhododendron along the side of the house, and the front door is propped open, multicolored disco lights flashing in time with the truly horrifically loud music being pumped throughout the neighborhood—it's like everything I'd originally imagined and nothing like I'd actually thought would be *real*.

This is, I suspect, an infamous Mena Dresden woods party.

Evie manages to find an open spot on the curb, and I get out slowly and wait for her to round the bumper.

She says, "I should have brought Tamara," slightly breathless.

In the middle of the stone walk, next to a little garden flag that says WELCOME, is Bern. He's not wearing a shirt. It's somewhat distracting. The tattoo of the purple octopus is even more amazing than I thought it would be, tentacles swirling up on his shoulder and curling over his heart. The flickering lights throw shadows over the curves of his muscles. His jeans are low enough on his hips to really drive home the tautness of his belly. I have no idea what's happening right now; I feel like I'm being strangled by invisible forces of hotness.

"Um," I say, throat dry. "Hi."

"Yo," he says, eyes crinkled up in this smile that has no business being on his face. His extremely naked and glorious shoulders are loose, and when I get close enough he wraps an arm around my back and I realize he's totally drunk.

He gives me this weird hug where he presses his face into my neck for a brief hot and sweaty moment. My heart makes a valiant effort to keep beating, and then he's ushering me inside.

I glance helplessly back at Evie, but she's already distracted by some sort of drum circle, oh my god, what kind of party is this?

It's wall-to-wall packed inside, and Bern drags me through to the kitchen with a hand on my wrist. It's so loud my brain is pulsing; there's just one wave of *music-singing-voices* that's nearly indistinguishable.

Bern pushes a red Solo cup into my hands, leans forward, and shouts, "Beer!" into my ear.

Mena, hair at maximum afro, a tiny scrap of a shirt around her boobs, presses me into a full body hug.

I nod hello to Hinkey and Zamir over her shoulder. The creepy-crawly sensation on the back of my neck makes me think Gia's lurking nearby with a hatchet or a pool cue or something, but a cursory glance around doesn't find her.

Mena pulls back and says, "You made it!" and also, "Bern was worried"—which, what?

Bern's hot hands find my arms again, peeling me out of Mena's grip.

He says, "Come on, it's better outside."

———

Better is relative, but outside has:

A patio with lounge chairs. Bowls of chips and cheese puffs. A kiddie wading pool filled with suspect liquid. The infamous bonfire, which is actually just a fire pit with sticks for roasting hot dogs and s'mores. Slightly less pounding bassline from the stereo.

Bern's skin looks golden in the firelight.

He makes himself comfortable on a lounger and gestures for me to come closer. I hesitate just long enough for someone to hand him an acoustic guitar. Oh my god.

"Oh my god," Evie says, sliding up next to me. She grips the side of my T-shirt.

Bern strums a chord, and people settle down around him—the drum circle sprawls in the grass, I spot a second guitar and a goddamn kazoo.

"Oh my god," Evie says again, the words hissed under her breath. She twists her fist, straining the seams of my shirt.

Bern opens his mouth and says, "Who wants to hear about prime numbers?" and the whole yard goes up in cheers.

Math songs.

Bern and his friends spend a whole half hour singing *math songs.*

Hands in my pockets, I clear my throat awkwardly. I say, "That was pretty bad."

"I know, right?" Bern says. He's grinning like he thinks what I really meant to say was *that was amazing.*

I've never been part of a sing-along about the Pythagorean Theorem. Or geometry shapes and the numbers of colors. "Are you a secret nerd?"

He scratches a hand over the octopus on his heart. "Not a very good one."

I'm losing my train of thought. There's sweat along his collarbone. "Not a very good secret, or not a very good nerd?"

He shrugs. "Both, probably. Wanna go make out in the upstairs hallway?"

I nearly swallow my tongue. "What?"

He crooks a finger, flashing teeth, and I end up following him back inside and up the steps like a puppy.

The hallway upstairs is narrow, with a single bathroom at the end, so anyone trying to use it will have to squeeze past where Bern has me backed up against the wall.

He tugs on the front of my T-shirt and says, "Relax, man. It'd be weird if we didn't do this, right?"

Oh, I think. Must be another thing he does. Previously with Gia. Now, supposedly, with me.

"Shouldn't we be doing our own stuff?" I say, shuffling closer as he reels me in, his other hand pressing on the small of my back. "You know, maybe some shit you *didn't* do with your ex-girlfriend?" My hands fall loose around his hips.

He breathes out noisily. "You think we did Art Buddies together? Got *coffee*?"

I actually have no idea. "Maybe?"

He noses the patch of skin just behind my ear and my breath catches. He says, "Tell you what. You let me know when you're working, and I'll stop by and hang. And we'll do our homework after school on Monday at the picnic tables in the courtyard."

"Make it after school on Tuesday," I say, tipping my head a little to the side. SASAC is on Monday, Evie would probably hurt me if I ditched her for a fake date.

"Tuesday," he agrees easily, arms now on either side of mine, bent to wriggle his fingers through my hair. He holds up my ponytail holder in front of my face with a triumphant grin. I hadn't even felt him yank it out.

"So you've never done homework with Gia?" I ask.

"Gia's aiming for early admission to Princeton. She does homework in a bubble with her phone turned off." Our lips are nearly touching. I can smell beer and cinnamon, like he's been chewing gum. "Now," he says, "can we stop talking about Gia?"

"I don't know," I say faintly—is he going to *actually* kiss me?—"Can we?"

He takes a deep breath; we're so close our chests press together. I watch his eyes, dark in the almost-nonexistent light. His impossibly long lashes sweep down and up in a slow blink. It feels like forever and no time at all before his arms slide down mine, elbows neatly leveraging me a healthy two steps away without doing any actual pushing. I almost *feel* like I've been kissed, even though our mouths never touched.

He says, "I think we're good now," and turns back down the hallway to walk away.

It was, upon reflection, one of the oddest nights I've ever had, and that includes the time Tom and Daphne had an impromptu lip-sync battle with an entire Justin Timberlake album.

"It's weird to have a crush on Bern, right?" I ask Evie in the car on the way home.

"No," Evie says. "It's not weird. It's completely tragic."

I slouch down in the seat with a groan. I'm pretty sure it was just the guitar, and the way Bern's tattoos were wearing his arms. His moonlight-gilded skin, sweet singing voice, and long, calloused artist fingers. I'm doomed.

"What exactly is supposed to happen here, though?" she asks.

"We go to Prom," I say, internally squaring my shoulders. This is what's going to happen, regardless. "Daphne will see me as a teenager who has definitely been kissed by another person. Our relationship will fade out in the summer heat. It'll all turn out just fine."

"Just fine," Evie says, and I don't think I'm imagining her skepticism.

I can acknowledge the odds of that happening are slim, but my best friend should be supporting my delusions.

"You're the literal worst," I say.

"You love me."

"Well, *yeah*." Duh.

Eleven

I wake up Monday morning to find a countdown to Prom taped to my bedroom door. There's a similar one on Daphne's that says GRADUATION, with something that could either be multicolored tears or fireworks sprouting off a stick figure with jazz hands.

Daphne herself is standing in the middle of the hallway, frowning. She says, "I'm not sure I feel confident enough in your future," in a way that makes me think she's either already been up for hours, or just never went to bed at all. Her hands are twitching.

Today I'll go to school. There's a 60 percent chance of a new dick being drawn on my locker, and a 90 percent chance of getting a shuttlecock to the face during gym. I might pretend to make out with Bern at some point. If I'm lucky, I'll get some sweet hand-holding out of it.

This is all fine. The only alarming thing is that all the Bern stuff is starting to feel normal.

Daphne doesn't know any of this, though. I look at her and say, "Why?"

She narrows her eyes. "Gia Hooper," she says, then whips a sheaf of papers out of nowhere—was she hiding that under her shirt?—and shoves the stack at my nose.

"What?" I manage to wrestle them out of her hand to see . . . a bundle of what looks like threatening notes, loose-leaf paper with neat square creases on them. "How did—where did these come from?"

"I've been taking them off your bike," she says, unconcerned. "I didn't want to upset you."

"Why are you upsetting me now, then?" I ask, flipping through the papers. It's—it could be worse, honestly. Most of them are just variations on *Treat him right or I'll squeeze your head like a lemon.* None of them are actually signed, but I can't think of anyone else who'd want to kill me. Right now.

She waves at the Prom countdown. "May eleventh is just around the corner! You've got about three weeks—"

Oh god, *three weeks*. Shouldn't I have a tux by now?

"—I figured she might escalate. You need to be prepared."

"She's not going to escalate." She might escalate.

Daphne waggles a finger in my face. "Your argument does not stand, baby bird."

"I have no argument," I say. "I just don't get the impression that Gia's into actual murder." I hope.

"Murder is the least of our worries," she says ominously. She rubs her palms together. "Leave it all to me."

———

Because Daphne is a crazy person, there's a high probability of her starting an imaginary feud with Gia that could end up with one or both of them dead. Or maimed. I have horror-filled visions of Daphne going at Gia with a field hockey stick and Gia fighting back with a flamethrower. There's zero I can do about it, though. Daphne will just ignore me anyhow, and Gia apparently thinks I'm the worst.

In our short, always fun-filled SAP meeting, Daphne shoves three more worksheets at me, slaps a good job sticker on the back of my hand for "surviving" GSA, and gives me a practice essay that, on a cursory look, is about werewolves.

Daphne says, "SATs are in *June*, baby bird." She leans over to poke at my belly. "And you've been doing suspiciously well on your math sheets."

I curl into my seat to avoid her sharp nails. Maybe I should get Bern to dumb it down a little.

When the bell rings, I escape the library and her judging eyes as fast as possible only to hide in the second-floor boys' bathroom. I feel like, after the morning I've had, I deserve to skip gym. I'm pretty sure Coach is going to give me at least a B just to avoid me telling Marla and Tom exactly how many times I've gotten hit in the head.

It takes me a moment to register that something is different about the bathroom: The window is wide open and the screen is popped out. Huh.

Cautiously, I poke my head outside. There's nothing below but the small, Y-shaped courtyard in between the science and foreign-language wings, and a couple of picnic tables and benches nestled between two big oaks. It's completely deserted at this time of the morning.

Twisting to look up, I see the bottoms of a pair of sneakers. The sneakers are attached to jean-clad legs. I stare at the dirty, ragged hems for a long, befuddled moment before saying, "How did you even get up there?"

I suspected they had a way up onto the roof out this window, but at the same time I didn't think there actually was a way up onto the roof out this window.

The legs part and I get dizzy just watching Zamir tip forward to look down at me. He frowns. "Do you solemnly swear you're up to no good?"

The Harry Potter reference throws me. "Uh . . . no?"

"Eh, whatever," he says, and then a rope ladder hits me in the face.

There are several problems with this situation, the smallest of which is the fact that everyone in the classrooms across the courtyard can probably see us, even with two tall leafy trees in the way. The biggest one is that I'm probably going to fall to my death.

"How is this secured?" I say, tugging at it.

Next to Zamir, Bennett pokes his head over the edge, dangling his arms. He does jazz hands and says, "Magic."

I flip him off, take a deep breath, and scramble out the window without looking down. It's not like I'm afraid of heights—I'm practically a skyscraper all by my lonesome—but I'd rather not be able to imagine how many tree limbs I'd hit if the rope slipped its "magic" hold and I fell.

I'm covered in cold sweat by the time I heave myself onto the roof. Triumph floods over my panic, though, and I just barely resist raising my hands in a victory shout. Plopping down on my butt, I say, "There is no way you guys haven't been caught doing this before. I don't get it."

Zamir and Bennett give me matching unimpressed looks.

Zamir holds up a finger as the second bell rings for first period, then rolls into a sprawl across the roof and pops open a ratty umbrella to block the sun. "Practice," he says, throwing an elbow over his eyes.

Bennett lies down on his stomach, chin propped in his hands. "Dude," he says, "it's all in the timing. Now flatten out so they can't see you at an angle."

"This is so dumb," I say. And uncomfortable. The rough roof coating is grating my skin as I move around. Is this supposed to be fun?

The sun is hot, even for spring, and there are damp patches in the dips of the roof from an overnight rain. I can smell the grease from the cafeteria lunch prep. I'm starting to think I'd have been better off just going to gym. Bennett is staring at me, I can feel it.

"What?" I finally say, throwing him an agitated glance.

He's rolled over on his side, squinting at me. "I'm trying to figure out what Bern sees in you," Bennett says, bringing one hand up to shade his eyes.

I bite my lip. It's a good question. "Okay."

Bennett nods and says, "Like, I get that the long hair is doing it for him—"

I tuck the mess that's fallen out of my ponytail behind my ears self-consciously.

"But you're kind of an asshole."

"I'm—" I swallow down a surprised laugh. I'm kind of an asshole? Since *when*? I've got the heart of a baby giraffe with the spindly legs to match.

Zamir laughs a little. He says, "He's not an asshole—"

"*Thank* y—"

"He's just pretentious. Pompous?" He lifts up his elbow so I can see his eyes, sparkling with humor. "I guess 'ass' goes hand in hand with that, though, right?"

"I'm not pretentious," I say.

"You created your own art club because the rest of us didn't 'get you,'" Zamir says, using honest-to-god air quotes.

"That was Evie."

Zamir quirks an eyebrow and says, "You refuse to take

Purdy's advice about anything because you think you're already a master *artiste*."

"That's not—" I flail an arm. "Purdy loves you." Of course he'd see it that way; Purdy kisses the easel Zamir's magnificent hand graces every day.

"Yeah, because when I'm stuck I ask her for help and actually listen to what she has to say." Zamir props himself up on his elbows, expression suddenly serious. "Look, I think what Benny's trying to say is that he's probably gonna punch you in the nuts if you hurt Bern."

My face flushes, and I'm not entirely sure if it's from anger or embarrassment. Still, in a small voice, I say, "Gia's probably got that covered."

"Then I'll just have to wait in line," Bennett says. Bennett is thin, small, and wiry, but he looks determined, and there's a good chance he could crack my skull open like a melon.

"Fine," I say, body tense. "Now how the hell do we get down?"

———

My grumpy mood spreads out all over the rest of the day.

In art, I carefully watch the way Ms. Purdy interacts with everyone else in class. The way she directs Arlo's hand over his clay, nodding with a smile when he says, "Like this?" The way she brings out a different set of watercolors for Steph

Crane, and declares Mouse's watercolor of the summer fruit still life a masterpiece to get him to stop crying. The way she seems to set her shoulders before coming over to my station, like she's heading into battle.

I'm not *that* bad. Definitely. Even though I've been having trouble with the coloring on the kiwi.

For the first time I notice the slight hesitancy in her voice when she says, "You know, Nolan, a little sunshine yellow never hurt anyone."

I don't need yellow. I just need to stop drawing vegetables and fruit. I sigh a little, though, because maybe Zamir is right—it's worth a shot. I say, "Okay," and feel a little buzz of warmth at her visible jolt of surprise.

Evie shoots me a wide-eyed look and Zamir smirks at me. I hate everyone.

Bern, set up next to me, pushes his foot into mine. He says, "Going soft, Grant?" and, crap, maybe I *am* an asshole? Do I have a reputation? I feel like I would have realized that before now if that was the case. Maybe. It's hard to hear things over the sound of Daphne winning and the collective Sheffield ego. Maybe that's *why*.

Double crap and damn.

I'm hyperaware, later that day, of the fact that we named our art club the Secret Awesome Sacred Art Club, and that we never invited anyone else to join.

We take a plate of Tom's snickerdoodles out to the patio and I ask, "Am I an asshole?"

Evie pats the back of my hand. "You're a sweetheart," she says.

"I *know*," I say, vindicated, and then Evie shrugs a little and says around a cookie, "You're a little bit of an ass, though."

"What? *No*." I am a gentleman in all things. Mostly.

She says, "You laughed in Arlo's face when he wanted to join SASAC."

"I—" I close my mouth with a click. I did. I'd totally forgotten about that. To be fair, Arlo was the main reason we started this club to begin with. "Okay, but does that really make me an asshole?" I say. "Bern's friends think I'm an asshole."

"Oh yeah." Missy is stalking across the backyard with her date blouse on.

Gator appears out of nowhere behind us and snags a handful of cookies. He says, "Hey, Nolan and Nolan's friend," with a salute.

Missy's heels click up onto the stone patio. Her skirt swishes around her legs; the sight is briefly mesmerizing. She says, "Bern's friends are looking out for Bern, and you basically humiliated him your freshman year."

"What are you talking about?" I say, shrinking under her wide, satisfied grin.

"Wait, what?" Evie says. She's perked up, sitting on the edge of her seat. "He did?"

"He asked you out and you yelled at him to leave you alone. That's what makes this so great," Missy says, rubbing her hands together like a cartoon villain. "His friends are going to eat you alive when you fuck this up."

Gator knocks a fist into my shoulder; I'm so stunned I let it rock me. He says, "Well, maybe you won't?" but even he, practically a stranger, doesn't sound super convinced.

"No, wait." I can't believe we're even having this conversation. "He was *bullying* me, I'm pretty sure I was in the right on that one."

Evie has her mouth half covered, eyes wide. "No. No, Missy's right. Oh my god, it makes so much more sense now."

"It doesn't," I say. I mean, why would Bern actually ask me out *for real*. It was definitely bullying. Of some sort. Right? I'd just come out, overly tall, greasy, *fourteen*, and he'd been so aggressive about, uh, going for pizza or whatever. And he's not even gay. I point at her and say, "You can't take his side on that one. I cried." I'd hid in the bathroom and sobbed into Evie's shoulder. It really wasn't my best moment.

Missy looks even more delighted at that revelation. Gator just looks uncomfortable.

He says, "Sorry, dude."

"Okay, you know what? I don't want to talk about this anymore." How much, honestly, can Missy Delgado, my archnemesis, actually be believed?

Missy winks at me before disappearing into the house.

I pull the plate of snickerdoodles closer and contemplate suffocating myself with crumbs.

My day ends with Daphne crawling in through my window at midnight. Apparently scaling the sides of buildings is going to be a *thing* now. I don't even bother asking her how she did it.

She's dressed head to toe in black, has a pair of binoculars looped around her neck, and the beginnings of a black eye that I'd be more worried about if I didn't know that she'd gotten elbowed in the face during a pickup game of basketball that afternoon.

"What's going on?" I say.

"What's going on is that Gia Hooper is boring," she says, dropping down into my desk chair, "but I'm not going to let that fool me."

"Were you—" I send a silent prayer for strength and fortitude toward my ceiling. "Were you spying on her all night?"

Daphne ticks off her fingers. "Homework right after school, dinner with her little brother and mom, watched *Mars*, fell asleep with a physics book draped on her chest— *boring*. You'd think someone who drives a motorcycle to school would be involved in one hundred percent more knife fights."

"Why were you spying on Gia?"

"Know thy enemy, Nolan! Even if she's apparently dull as a spoon."

"She's not my enemy," I say.

Daphne throws her hands up. "Of course she is. She's a threat to your happiness, baby bird, and that makes her the enemy. You don't think she might try to weasel her way back into Bern's pants? She stares at you like she wants to explode your head with her apparently enormous brain. Now imagine," she says, softer, "trying to compete with over two years of dating. She knows Bern inside and out. If she sets her mind to it, you'd be flicked out of the picture like a ladybug."

I don't say that I don't actually have any kind of real hold on Bern anyway.

I swallow hard, the thought leaving a bitter taste in my mouth.

Twelve

Tuesday starts with me narrowly missing getting hit by a truck on my bike, so—business as usual.

Dick on my locker: check.

Daphne clucking her tongue over my insane werewolf SAT practice essay: check.

Hand-holding with Bern after English: check.

Si showing up at my lunch table: *weird*.

There is a span of time, maybe seconds, when everyone at the table freezes. Dave with his nose in a book, a fry halfway to his mouth. Missy with two fingers hovering over Dave's Froot Loop gummies. Carlos with a mouthful of cookies, paused mid-chew.

Daphne has her head cocked, like a curious puppy, and I'm slowly squeezing the life out of my peanut butter and jelly sandwich.

Si's either oblivious to the sudden quiet, or doesn't care. He just pulls out the chair next to Daphne and sets down his tray. He shakes his orange juice before peeling it open and grins at me. Daphne kicks my leg under the table. The general consensus is that Si is a nice guy, but that doesn't mean he makes a habit of appearing out of nowhere and sweeping a table of sideshows off their feet.

Daphne says pointedly, "Hello."

"Hey." Si turns his grin on her, knocking their shoulders together like they're sharing some kind of joke.

"Are you lost?" Daphne says.

"Nah." He shakes his head. "Just wanted to see Nolan."

She shoots me a look. *Missy* shoots me a look. There's a burning in my chest that feels like either embarrassment or acid reflux, and Dave clears his throat over his copy of *Jane Eyre*.

Si nods at me. He says, "Thanks for your help this weekend. I really think the sale is gonna be extra awesome this year."

Extra awesome, Missy mouths, like Si is a space alien or talking horse.

We make it through most of lunch with light conversation, though, and I try not to stare too much at his bare forearms.

And then Adrian Fells passes behind our table on his way to the trash cans. I tense up. He's left us physically alone for the most part, spreading ugly gossip that Daphne's refused to let any of us react to—apparently that just fuels the machine even more—but he's glaring at the back of Daphne's head now.

I feel like I know it's coming before it happens, a ball of rage and dread forming in the pit of my stomach.

Adrian says, "Hey, no need for a doggie bag when Daphne Sheffield's around, right?" He laughs meanly, says, "Woof," and tips his half-eaten plate of spaghetti over Daphne's shoulder. Because he's a monster. It splatters on the table, hitting Si's arm and half his body, and Daphne startles up out of her seat on a gasp, swiping frantically at her lap with her napkin.

Missy *growls*. I want to rip Adrian's head off and stuff it backward down his neck, but I'm also too stunned by the fact that he actually *dumped his plate on Daphne* to do anything but stare.

"What the hell?" Si says.

It's obvious that Adrian hadn't noticed the guy sitting next to Daphne was Si O'Mara. Si pushes back his chair and stands up, watery red sauce soaking his T-shirt, and my welling rage eases some as Adrian goes sickly pale.

"Sorry, dude," Adrian says, hands up and chest out. "Didn't see you. What are you doing at the freak table?"

"*That's* your problem?" Si says, brow furrowed. "Not that you called Daphne a dog?"

Adrian smirks. "If it walks like a—"

Si holds up a hand to stop him and says, visibly

disappointed, like he somehow expected more from *Adrian Fells*, "Bro. Man. Apologize to the lady."

Adrian opens and closes his mouth silently. Finally, he says, "Are you serious?" like he's genuinely bewildered. Like being a decent person is totally beyond him. Honestly, it probably is.

Si shakes his head. "Wow, not cool, Fells." He looks down at Daphne, places a hand lightly on her arm, and says, "Are you okay?"

"Sure. Red's totally my color." Daphne's eyes have a shine of tears over them that she'd never let drop, but she's smiling up at Si like he hung the moon.

Si grins back. "We'll match."

"Fuck off, O'Mara," Adrian says, incredulous.

Si ignores him and tells Daphne, "I'll get us more napkins."

Si is . . . *freaking adorable*, that's the only thing I can think of right now, staring over at him joking good-naturedly with Daphne about getting food dumped all over them.

Missy says, "What was that?" when Adrian and his friends finally slink away.

"I just want everyone to be chill, you know?" Si says. "Fells can be an asshole."

"Fells *is* an asshole," Missy says, like she still can't figure Si out.

Daphne just says, "Thanks," though. "Thank you, that was perfect."

136

It really was. I'm in awe of his de-escalation powers. It's like he doesn't even realize how amazing that was. If he hadn't been here, Missy probably would have tried to claw Adrian's eyes out and everyone would have gotten suspended.

Si's face looks a little flushed, but he just shrugs and says, "Sure."

Daph wrinkles her nose and plucks at her shirt. She says, "At least I still have my hockey bag in my locker." Which means she can change into her jersey, even though I'm pretty sure she hasn't brought that home to be washed since her last game months ago.

"Same, but with football. Matching jerseys, dude," Si says, and holds his hand out for a fist bump.

———

Bern is lounging by my locker after the last bell.

I fumble with my lock, and he just smirks at me.

"All right there, Grant?" he says.

He's got his satchel crossed over his chest and his hands tucked in his pockets. His jeans are stuffed into the tops of his boots, his hair is gelled up into a faux-hawk, and he should look stupid, but he totally doesn't. He's got badass nonchalance down to an art form.

"Fine," I say. "Courtyard?"

Bern nods, then holds out a hand. I stare down at it, momentarily thrown, until he wiggles his fingers and I realize he expects me to reach out, too. There's a rush of students around us doing their best to get out of the school as fast as possible. It's not that big a deal, we do this practically every day after English, but the change in routine kicks my heart up into my throat—and then his smirk softens and I roll my eyes and thread our fingers together.

This is good. This is something *we* do, not Bern and Gia. Bern and Gia didn't hold hands, and they didn't do homework together, and this is good in all ways except the one where this makes things feel more real than fake.

"So," Bern says as we push out the doors into the inner courtyard. "You and O'Mara?"

"No," I say. "I mean. What?"

He shakes off my suddenly tight grip and takes a seat at a picnic table, swinging his bag up. "Z said O'Mara sat with you at lunch today. And he *did* ask you to join the GSA."

"Well, yeah," I say, sitting down across from him. It's a little odd, maybe, but there's no me and Si. That's ridiculous.

He shrugs, pulls out *Beowulf.* I blink at the battered copy, because I'm pretty sure Bern has never before done our assigned English reading.

"I just figured—" Bern says, then stops and curls the paperback up in his hands. He stares down at the table for a long second—a patch of afternoon sun falling through the oak leaves makes one entire side of his face shine bright gold—and then back up at me. "Is that your endgame here?"

"What?"

"I thought this was to get Sheffield off your back about Prom, but hey," he jabs the book toward me, "landing O'Mara would be pretty sweet, right?"

I can't say no, and for some reason I don't want to say yes.

Bern nudges the end of his book at my knuckles. When I look up at him, he just says, "Homework."

"Right," I say, nodding. I'm hoping if I look hopeless enough at my trig homework he'll offer to help me out.

———

I'm almost entirely sure Gia eats a bowlful of baby bunny hearts every morning for breakfast, even though Daphne insists, from her Wednesday morning surveillance, that all Gia actually has is plain oatmeal with raisins sprinkled in it.

"Her nine-year-old brother is more interesting," Daphne says, lying back on top of my bed after school. "He has hamsters."

"Okay."

She holds up her hands and spreads her fingers out, squinting up at the ceiling light. "Let's not talk about Gia, though—"

"You're the one that keeps bringing her up!" I throw my hands out, straightening up from my slump in my desk chair.

"—let's talk about what you've got planned for the Under the Sea After Prom."

"Uh." My fingers curl into fists, dropping to my thighs. There's a chance I've got nothing planned at all. I might have forgotten about it. Oops.

Daphne says, "I'm sure you'll think of something amazing," before dramatically heaving herself off the bed to go see if dinner is ready yet.

I stare after her blindly, wondering if it's possible to die from panic-related anxiety.

Five hours later, I have the massacred remains of a painted paper bottlenose dolphin all down my front and very little else to show for it.

I don't even bother to look through the peephole when someone knocks on the front door. It's creeping up on 1 A.M., and I probably look like I've eaten and then thrown up a Smurf. I welcome death, if it's come for me.

Bern has his hand up, mid-knock, when I yank it open.

He's got a backpack on his shoulder, leather jacket thrown over what is clearly an old T-shirt and sleep pants. I blink blearily at the tiny seahorse print on them. He looks soft all over, and I have to fight the urge to pull him into a hug and close my eyes against his shoulder.

"Did I panic text you?" I ask, half-heartedly swiping paint off my face. I texted Evie, too, but all she sent back was a crying-laughing emoji.

Bern holds up his phone—there are three full lines of exclamation points on the screen, did I fall asleep at one point? Stroke out?—and says, "I think you're overthinking this."

Right now I'm working on using iridescent streamers, a clear plastic bowl, and a soft white light bulb to somehow create a jellyfish. I should probably involve someone who knows how to wire things and will stop me from accidentally electrocuting myself.

My ideas are sound, okay. I just need to practice practical execution.

I'm not exactly sure how long I've been staring at Bern, angelic in the hallway light, before I wrinkle my nose and ask, "Do you think Linz knows how to wire a lamp?" Linz is good at arson, isn't that practically the same thing?

"Linz can make soy candles and set the chemistry room on fire," Bern says, squinting down at my mess. "But maybe you should concentrate on something that might not accidentally burn down the school gym. Have you thought of battery-operated twinkle lights?"

I stare at him in awe. "What?" I say, and he's already unzipping his bag, pulling out strands of fairy lights. "Oh my god," I breathe. "Bern, you're my hero."

His face has a weirdly soft smile. "Sure," he says, like he doesn't quite believe me.

"You are." He's definitely my savior tonight; this is *amazing*. I grab for the lights and hug them to my chest and say, "Thank you," with sincere, crazed enthusiasm. My energy reserves are dwindling. Collapsing is probably eminent, but I've got no time for sleep.

Cool lighting idea: check. Now I just need to convince Arlo to help me build a giant papier-mâché shark that we can hang from the ceiling, somehow create a giant reef made out of sponges or Styrofoam or plywood in the middle of the room, and have all the walls covered in floating seaweed, along with fish peeking out here and there.

Bern shrugs a little, dipping his head. There's a flush on the tops of his cheeks that I kind of want to press my thumbs to. Thank god my hands are full.

"Can I help with anything else? Uh." Bern turns in place, looking around. There are discarded piles of papers that have cartoon narwhals all over them with "go fuck yourself" thought bubbles over their heads. "Maybe you should just call it a night."

"I need to figure out woodworking," I say. It can't be that hard, right? I've got some knives. "I should probably clean up."

"That'll keep until you can see straight enough not to cut your hands open on a pair of scissors," Bern says, catching my arm as I stumble.

Ignoring his warmth all up and down my side, I try to pretend that I'm not leaning heavily into him.

He steers me toward the bottom of the stairs with a hand on my back. The house is dark and quiet around us, and I roll my shoulders, feeling his fingers shift over my T-shirt.

"I'm good," I say, gripping the bottom of the railing.

He drops his hand and backs up, and I watch him step carefully toward the front hallway. His backpack is still half-open, dangling from his left hand, straps dragging on the carpet.

I say, "Thanks," again, and he waves silently before slipping out the door.

In my room, I tug out my phone and see all the texts I'd sent him. Not just the exclamation points, but also: *pls hlp me save gsa* and *du kno any practical lighting solutions* and *narwhals hav a tooth nt a horn* with five smiley faces after it.

I groan and flop back on my bed and think about how I should probably shower, but instead I fall asleep with the overhead light on, still covered in paint.

Thirteen

I don't actually fully wake up the next day until Plank hits me in the face with a beanbag hard enough to split my lip open during gym.

Coach throws up his hands in exasperation.

In the locker room, Bern's friend Hinkey says, "This is harassment, right? Why hasn't Plank or Sid or Small Tony been sent to the principal's office yet?" in some weird bid to defend my honor, which basically only makes Small Tony mad that someone is actually calling him Small Tony out loud.

Tossing the bloody paper towels in the wastebasket, I spit into the sink and wonder if I should go to the nurse or not. I'm gonna get a fat lip either way. I poke at the sluggishly bleeding cut with my tongue, and then Hinkey appears in the mirror behind me and holds up a first aid kit.

Hinkey's been in my gym class the entire semester; it's a little weird to see him showing all this concern all of a sudden.

I clean up the wound with an antiseptic pad while he waves a bandage in the air. "Think a butterfly will hold it?"

"Eh. Probably not." It'd get too wet around my mouth. More trouble than it'd be worth.

A throat clears off to my right, and I glance over to see Bern staring at me, head cocked, one eyebrow up. His expression is a cross between amused and concerned. "You look like you lost a fight with a beanbag."

Hinkey says, "It wasn't as funny as it sounds."

"It doesn't sound funny at all," I grumble, and glare ineffectually over at Bern. "Why are you here?"

All I can picture is his sleep-mussed hair and pajama pants from the night before, and I fight down a rising blush. That actually happened. Crap.

"Thought I'd walk you to English," Bern says. The bell rings a second warning and he slumps into an obviously practiced lounge against the bank of lockers. I don't understand how he can look so cool and also like he's falling asleep at the same time. "Or we can skip it."

"Evie'll skin me," I say. She won't, actually, she'll just want to know all the details on why.

"We should just skip the whole day," Hinkey says, snapping the first aid kit shut.

Bern turns a questioning look on me.

"The school would call my dad," I point out. It's like—have a couple dozen truancy notices sent to the group home from middle school, and your whole life is suddenly on red alert for forever. School transcripts expire at some point, right?

Coach's bodiless voice echoes throughout the locker room: "My blind eye only turns so far, boys."

Hinkey says, "I'm pretty sure at this point Grant can sue you, Coach."

There's a pause. And then: "Fair enough. Carry on."

Hinkey always seemed like a dumbass. A hulking mass of bad decisions, unfortunate facial hair, and a whistle that hangs onto his *s*'s like he's missing a tooth. He smiles at me now and all I can see are the crinkled edges of his eyes and the way his cheeks puff out like rosy apples framed by muttonchops.

He says, "C'mon, NGS. If you don't want to skip, I bet Coach'll write us a late note."

"Okay?" I figured maybe there'd be more calling me a wuss or something for not wanting to skip. Chicken clucking. Derisive laughter?

Bern salutes me with two fingers and says, "I'll still walk you to class."

I'm *this close* to talking Evie into going to GSA with me after school—she has her exasperated-maybe face on, like she might give in just to shut me up—when Parker Montgomery the Third rocks into my side, pushing me up against my locker.

I think for a second he's trying to knock me over, but then he loops an arm around my waist and shouts, "Walruses!"

Evie snorts. She says, "I'll meet you at Art Buddies," and scuttles away like a coward. Ugh.

"Um. What." I try to scrape him off, but he's surprisingly strong for a dude sporting a popped collar.

He waves his free arm around. "Fucking ugly flop bulls of the sea. They're totally fucking awesome."

"Flop bulls?" I echo. I'm having a hard time figuring out where Parker is going with this.

"We're all excited to see what you've come up with for After Prom," he says, shaking my whole body before finally letting me go. He walks backward down the hall, giving me finger guns.

I stare after him, frowning, and then say to no one in particular—the drab, painted concrete walls, the faded narwhal drawn on the ceiling above my locker that the administration hasn't seemed to notice yet—"Do you think he's just fucking with me?"

"Oh yeah," someone says.

I flick a glance across the hall to where Linz Garber is zipping up her backpack. "Yeah?"

She grins at me. "Let me know if you want me to set him on fire."

In no world should Linz Garber be joking about setting stuff on fire. I'm alarmed but unsurprised. I nod and say, "Will do," anyway.

Grabbing my sketch pad and the plastic bag holding my mock-up of the jellyfish light out of my locker, I reluctantly make my way down the hall after Parker.

The home ec room is filled to the brim with eager ninth graders and the scent of fresh-baked cookies. Si presides over everyone with a wide grin. He waves an oven-mitted hand and says, "Settle down, kids, there's enough for everyone," as I slink into the back of the room.

It's like the entire GSA club doubled over the course of a week, except once the freshmen have handfuls of cookies clutched in their fists, they start slowly trickling out. On the one hand, I'm relieved. On the other, it's taking forever for the meeting to actually get started, since as some kids leave, more make their way in. Clusters of giggling fifteen-year-olds jam up the doorway.

And then Parker Montgomery the Third climbs up onto a chair and shouts, "Extras, out! Be gone, tiny monsters!" He points at me over the crowd and says, "Yo, art dude, show us what you've got."

All but four of the freshmen hurry up and leave, slamming the door behind them. Everyone stares at me. I clutch my bag to my chest and glare at Parker, but he just bares his teeth in a parody of a smile and hops down from his chair.

It's a little disconcerting having so many eyes focused on me, but the "oohs" and "aahs" of appreciation when I snick on my jellyfish light are deeply gratifying.

"This is just the prototype," I say. "I think if we can get someone from robotics involved with the lighting—get it to mimic movement?—it could be cool."

Parker, who has somehow migrated to my side on cat feet, drapes an arm across my shoulder and says, "I'm reluctantly impressed, art dude," and I feel a tiny pang of guilt that I didn't mention how much Bern helped.

"Stop calling me art dude." I try to shrink away from him, but then Si bookends me on the other side. I'm trapped between a wall of muscle and a guy in a pastel shirt with a little alligator over his heart.

Si takes the jellyfish out of my hands and turns it upside down and around, whistling softly between his teeth. "Awesome," he says, grinning. "So cool."

Only Si O'Mara could express that level of pure enthusiasm over a lighting fixture and not sound like a tool.

My cheeks prickle with heat. "It might not even work," I say. "We'd have to figure out how to get them to hang from the gym ceiling."

"What's this?" Tasha says, flipping uninvited through

my sketchbook. It's open to a shark spanning the width of two pages, and I shrug Parker off to step up next to her.

I say, "It's a giant shark," and manage to bite back a pissy *duh*.

She hums under her breath, one sharp pink nail tapping on the picture. Her mouth is pressed together in either some form of concentration or total disappointment.

In the quiet, I hastily say, "Same problem here, though: How would we hang it?"

"What, a giant 3-D shark? Is that what you're saying?" Parker asks, spinning the paper away from Tasha to hold it up in front of himself.

"Papier-mâché," I say. "Arlo might help."

"Okay," Si says, nodding. "Okay, these are some really great ideas." He makes his way back up to the front of the room and the whiteboard, uncapping a green marker. He says, "Now let's talk about the plant sale on Sunday, and how much we think we can budget for decorations, and who wants to sneak another basket of condoms into the career lounge."

———

The overabundance of cookie-hungry freshmen, combined with a lengthy argument over how conspicuous Mykos would be trying to smuggle condoms into the career lounge, make the meeting drag on well over the appointed hour. I finally leave the classroom with several exasperated texts from Evie on my phone when I don't show up for Art Buddies.

Included is a pic of what looks like a zombie apocalypse diorama.

Her last text, from five minutes ago, is weird: *Bern looks sad.*

I stare at it for several moments before texting back: *and you care why?*

Why should *I* care?

She hasn't replied by the time I get my bike unlocked. I stuff my phone into my back pocket and snap my backpack strap across my chest.

My phone vibrates as I pull out of the parking lot, but I wait until I'm safely on the other side of the pike to tug it out again.

It's not a text from Evie, though.

Under BERN on my lock screen are the words: *Gsa went long?*

Pressing down on the message to bring up the reply block, I waffle over what to say—Duh? Miss me? Evie says you're sad?—then type: *Yeah.*

He sends me back a smiling-face emoji with its tongue sticking out, and I snort-laugh out loud.

What even. God.

The grind of a poorly maintained engine idling and the distinct smell of smoldering felt pulls me from grinning stupidly down at my cell screen.

"Baby bird," Daphne shouts out the window of her piece of shit car. "Are you lollygagging on pizza and pie night?" The trunk pops open with a loud creak. "Haul ass, Nolan. Dad already has *Tiny House Nation* queued up."

Fourteen

Mim doesn't really say it outright, but I think she misses me when I skip Art Buddies.

On Friday, she says, "Kip's completely color blind, like a *dog*," and I take that as a blanket *everything sucks when you're not here* message. It's heartwarming.

And then she says, "I'm going to paint your face."

She has her short dark hair pulled back in two little pigtails, bangs held off to the side in a unicorn-shaped barrette, posing with her hip out, like a challenge. I eye the array of little jars of paints on our table. None of them, as far as I can see, are officially labeled for human skin.

I narrow my eyes at her and say, "Then I'm going to paint your face, too."

Holding out a hand, she says, "Deal," and that is how I end up with a butterfly mask on that probably won't actually come off.

Evie stands in front of me afterward and says, "What did you do?"

Mim looks like a clown; I think I got the better end of that deal.

Bern slinks up next to Evie and stares at me. He says, "I can't believe I'm going to be seen with you in public."

"Uh. Okay?" We didn't have any plans, but my other choices probably involve board games.

"Are the wings outlined in glitter?" he asks.

I have no idea, but I wouldn't be surprised. "It's certainly possible." The paint itches and I want to scrub my hands all over it, but it'll look way worse smudged. My fingers curl over my collar. "Where are we going?"

He flashes teeth when he smiles. "It's Friday," he says. "I'm taking you home to dinner."

———

Bern lives near Evie. This is the only thing that keeps me from totally freaking out, knowing that at least I'm not trapped there if something terrible happens. Evie's one street over, I can walk there and she can hold me while I cry.

"They won't care that I'm a guy?" I ask, looking up at the boxy, two-story house. *Or that I look like I just stepped out of a carnival.*

"Honestly, they'll probably care more that you're not Jewish," he says, plucking at my sleeve and jerking his head toward the front walk.

I stare at him without moving.

"I'm joking, Grant. You'll be fine." He looks far more impatient than I feel like this situation warrants, shifting back and forth on his feet. Is *he* nervous?

We should slow down. This is so stupid. "Why do I even have to meet your parents?" I ask, totally not whining. It doesn't matter what we actually do, so long as everyone *thinks* we're doing it.

The tops of Bern's cheeks color. "My cousins have big mouths."

"Cousins?" Just how many family members am I going to meet tonight? Ugh.

"You're lucky Mimsy and Bex like you." He frowns. "Kind of."

"*Mimsy*?" I say. Mimsy is the most ridiculous name I've ever heard, and I named my cat Fuzzbutt McGundersnoot. Then the rest of his words hit me. "Mim and Bex? *Art Buddies* Mim and Bex?" The fond disdain they seem to have for one another suddenly makes a lot more sense.

Bern sighs and shoves his hands in his pockets. "Mim thinks you're sort of cute." From the sour look on his face, I'm guessing those words taste wrong.

"Mim," I say. "Mim, yea high"—I lift my hand to the

middle of my chest—"likes to torture me with glitter and permanent marker?" Mim thinks I'm *cute*. No one's called me cute since I was twelve and grew six inches on every single one of my limbs practically overnight.

"Yeah," he says. He tilts his head back to look up at the sky. "She thinks it's hilarious that we're dating, by the way, so . . ." He shrugs again.

"So what you're saying," I say slowly, "is that we have to convince Mim and Bex that we're *really* dating."

"We have to convince Mimsy and Bex not to tell Gia I'm a loser," Bern says. "And I used to drag Gia to these dinners all the time."

Going into the Bernstein house just keeps getting more and more daunting. The sky behind it is creeping up on evening, deep purple bruises fanning out on either side, shadowing the roof and making it look dark and menacing.

Bern takes a deep breath. "Not gonna lie, Grant, my family's pretty hung up on Gia."

YOU'RE pretty hung up on Gia, I don't say. Because what would be the point? "Right," I say. This night is going to be so much fun.

And then a car pulls into the driveway and Mim and Bex spill out of the backseat and I have no choice but to square my shoulders and soldier on.

———

Bern doesn't have a huge family. I'm mostly grateful for this, even though having a bigger crowd might have taken some of the pressure off me.

I'm squished between Bern and Bex at the dinner table. Bern's parents are down at one end, his aunt and uncle on the other, with Mim and a gnarled, wrinkled elderly gentleman across from us, who I can only assume is a grandparent. He winks at me when we sit down and then spends the rest of the meal feeding Bern's dog—a nervous-looking brindle whippet named George—under the table.

Bern's mom keeps sending me weird little glances. Even though I spent the first five minutes in the house locked in the downstairs bathroom frantically scrubbing paint off my face, it could be because I still have glitter all over my cheeks. Or it could be because Bern introduced me as his *boyfriend.* That's, like, upping the game to one thousand.

Fake boyfriend. I clench and unclench my fingers around my fork. That's somehow so much more pressure.

I mean, we don't even have break-up plans. Oh god, I didn't know we'd need *break-up plans.*

I nearly spill my drink when Bern knocks our shoulders together. He leans down and whispers, "Stop looking like Pops is gonna eat you."

"Pops" bares his teeth in a smile. George's tiny black nose peeks over the edge of the table under his arm. Am I the only one who notices George snatching a piece of potato off Pops's plate?

Mr. Bernstein frowns and says, "So, Nolan. Aren't you the—"

"Mimsy says she works with Nolan in Art Buddies. You know, Sam," Bern's aunt says to Mr. Bernstein, "she's been so much more agreeable at home now."

Mim, ridiculous clown-face still proudly intact, sticks her tongue out at her mom, but her mom just grins back.

"Ira," Mrs. Bernstein says hesitantly, ignoring Mim's mom and darting her eyes between me and Bern, "are you sure about this?"

My ears heat. I stare fixedly at George as he snatches another piece of food off Pops's plate. He's basically in Pops's lap now; there's no way Pops doesn't know what's happening.

Mrs. Bernstein gives Bern a helpless look. "You were just so happy with—"

"Mom," Bern says. "No."

If they don't notice the dog, maybe no one would notice if I slid down and disappeared under the table.

And then Bex says, "My Art Buddy's a lesbian," idly licking at the tines of her fork, and Bern rubs his hand over his eyes and groans.

———

After dinner, we narrowly escape to Bern's room with a plateful of cookies. I'm unsure if this is an actual improvement on the evening—given that we're now in a room with a bed, and his mom had yelled up the stairs after us to leave the door open, oh my god—but at least Mim is no longer staring at me with a creepily knowing look on her face.

Bern's bedroom is small and cramped, with a messily made twin bed covered in blue plaid and a shelf full of trophies that, on closer inspection, are for being a mathlete.

There are posters for bands I've never heard of plastered all over the walls, and at least three of Fall Out Boy from the chubby Patrick Stump era. His single closet door is completely covered in bumper stickers. There's laundry spilling out of a wicker basket in the corner by a desk that looks like it isn't used as anything except a place to pile books. A corkboard hangs over it, just beside the double window—there are scraps of paper, pictures of his friends, Gia and him with their arms around each other. I feel weird staring at it and turn away to see him sprawled out on his bed.

His arms are bent over his head, pulling his shirt up so I can see the dark trail of hair above the waistband of his jeans. He does know the door is open, right? Clenching my hands together, I stare at the ceiling and count down from ten. When I look at him again, he's sitting up, arms resting on his thighs and hands between his knees, smirking.

Ass-hat, I think. Jesus.

"We should . . ." He makes a come-here motion, and I automatically back up a step.

"What. Here?"

"Yeah," he says, and when I absolutely refuse to move closer he gets to his feet.

"Uh." I walk backward until my back hits the door-frame, even though he hasn't made another move toward me. I can hear Mim and Bex giggling at the end of the hall. Bern's room is right at the top of the stairs. Anyone with eyes could just glance up and see us. "*Here?*"

"School bathrooms, parties, my bedroom, all places I've—"

"Didn't we talk about not doing everything you and Gia did?" I say, voice only a little on the high end. I mean. God. I really don't want to think about what Bern and Gia could have gotten up to in his *bedroom*. I tilt my head back against the wood frame and close my eyes. This is so embarrassing. Possibly if I'd had more experience with this sort of thing, I wouldn't be so terrible at faking it. When I open my eyes again, Bern's frowning at me.

"What's wrong?" he asks.

I sigh. "It's just weird," I say. "I mean, we haven't actually kissed, *I* haven't even . . ." I trail off, something hot strangling my windpipe; I can feel a flush steadily making its way up my throat.

"What are you saying?" Bern asks, slow.

"I'm not saying anything." My heart is beating so hard in my chest, I feel like he can see it. Sweat prickles out around my wrists, the small of my back. I'm lying through my teeth.

"No," Bern says. "You've really never . . . ? With any-one?"

I'm jittery, nervous. Bern slides closer with his eyes laser focused on my mouth, and I don't know if I'm panicking because I think he's going to kiss me, or because I think he *isn't*. I force my limbs to relax, swallow down the urge to laugh.

I say, "Well, it's almost like we have, right?" Are we still talking about kissing? I think we're still talking about kissing, but Bern smells like chocolate chip cookies and bad decisions, and he doesn't even have to reach up to press our mouths together.

His lips are warm and too dry until his hands find their way around my neck and he moves in closer.

He murmurs, "Relax," and my mouth falls open.

There's a buzzing in the back of my head and a tongue licking over my bottom lip, slick over my teeth, and every-thing is over and done way too quickly.

"There," he says, voice hoarse. He steps back, his arms dropping to his sides. This part is just like any other of our fake make-out sessions, the sudden distance, but my lips are damp and tingling and I have no idea what the fuck just happened.

"What?" I say. *What?*

He clears his throat. "Now you have. Kissed someone."

Oh. I clamp my teeth down on a hysterical laugh. I feel

tense and awkward, and also like I really want to kiss him again. "But, uh," I manage to say, "why?"

"Why what?" He looks genuinely puzzled.

"Why would you . . . ?" I flail a hand. "You're not gay."

He winces. "Nolan, seriously? I asked you out freshman year."

"But that . . . you dated Gia for two years!" I say. He can't be *gay*.

"And now I'm dating you," he says, only he's backed up even more, so he's half sitting on his desk, arms crossed in front of his chest. His face looks mutinous, chin tipped up. "I don't have to be gay to like guys."

"Okay, first of all, you're right," I say, straightening up to my full height. He's *right*. I just never thought he could be bi. Which is stupid, considering how okay he was with going with me to Prom.

Some of the defensiveness melts out of Bern's stance.

"Second of all," I say, because my mind keeps hopping toward the greater implication here, "does that mean you've never kissed a guy before?"

He frowns. He touches his fingers lightly to his mouth. "I just kissed you."

I shift on my feet. "Other than me," I say.

"*Other* than you," he shrugs, "there was Gia. And before that I was fourteen, five foot five, and had a buzz cut and braces. Even you didn't want me."

"Okay," I say, tensing up. Even me: the weird, gay,

adopted kid. Right. "Good thing we're not actually dating now, then."

He sighs, shoves a hand through his hair. "I didn't mean that the way it sounded."

I make a face. "You probably did." I don't even really feel mad about it. Just sort of sad. Once upon a time Bern might've liked me a little, but I was too much of a dick to notice.

"Look," he says, pushing off from the desk and moving toward me again. His sleeves are shoved up toward his elbows. I stare at the strain of muscles there, the way his wrists look tense, the sparse hair on the back of his hands. "You can fake being in a relationship, Grant." He looks gray, and I don't know what to do with that.

"Yeah," I say, only a little defensive.

He nods, stares out the open door of his room. After a weird, quiet moment, he sighs and says, "But it still feels like dating." He finally looks at me again, a small rueful smile on his lips. "Right?"

Fifteen

I wake up Saturday morning with imaginary tenderness on my mouth, hide in the bathroom for twenty minutes making sure it's *only* imaginary tenderness, and then escape the house with a to-go pancake and a pint of OJ that Tom lobs at my head as I run for the door.

Work starts out fine. Normal. Even if Mr. Talbot asks me if I'm okay at least fifteen times in the first hour alone.

And then there's brief but intense internal flailing when Bern shows up with lunch. I'd been semi-successfully avoiding thinking about Bern, and Bern's kiss, and the implication that we're in a fake relationship, but somehow not *actually* fake dating, and this is really putting a crimp in my plans for denial.

Mr. Talbot winks at me from behind a row of Japanese maples, like he's finally figured me out. My face heats, and I stare down at the hamburger Bern brought me and quietly think about dying.

Bern kicks my leg underneath the table and says, "What's up?"

What's up. So normal, like we didn't just suck face the night before. Like his mom didn't hug me goodbye before he drove me home, and like he didn't walk me all the way up to my fucking front door. God.

"Nothing," I say.

This is so awkward. This shouldn't be this awkward, right?

And then Bern looks up and freezes and says, "Don't freak out."

"Um. What?"

He puts his elbows on the table and leans toward me. "Think very carefully," he says. "When did your sister start hanging out with Gia?"

I'm . . . not sure I heard that right. "What?"

And then Daphne is dropping down onto the bench next to me and Gia is eyeing me from the head of the picnic table and I don't know what to do.

"Your sister has a high tolerance for pain, but the stealth of a water buffalo," Gia says.

Daphne says, "Hey!" at the same time that I say, "Did you guys *fight*?" checking Daphne over for any visible injuries.

I don't see anything that could be a machete wound or a flash burn, though, just a couple scrapes on her arms.

"She very noisily fell off my lattice," Gia says drily,

finally sitting down about as far from all of us as she can manage without being at a different table.

Bern says, "Why are you here?" He has his arms pulled in defensively. His eyes are wary.

"We're getting ice cream," Daphne says. "Do you boys want any?"

I share a *what the hell* look with Bern. He says, "But why are you *here*?"

Gia sighs and says, "Just so everyone's aware, I have not been sending Grant threatening messages—"

"What?" Bern says, whipping his gaze from Gia to me and then back again.

"Well, okay, maybe a *couple* were from me," she says, and she doesn't look sorry for that at all. "But I'm pretty sure most of them were from Benny. Bern's a big boy; he can take care of himself. And now that I've confessed all I know, this crazed lunatic," she hooks her thumb at Daphne, who smiles brightly back at her, "can stop creeping on my house."

"Can I come in and pet the hamsters?" Daphne says, and Gia says, adamant, "*No.*"

"Wait, Benny *what*?" Bern asks, talking over Daphne's disappointed, "Aw, shucks."

"It's fine," I say. I should have known they were from Bennett. He's the smallest and yet angriest of Bern's friends.

Daphne steals a handful of my fries. She knocks our elbows together and says, voice low, "I got your back," while across from us, Bern and Gia have a conversation that seems to take place entirely with their eyebrows.

Then Gia heaves to her feet and says, "Ice cream." She jerks her head at Daphne, not quite smiling. It's more like a grimace with a semi-genuine edge. "Let's go."

Behind Bern, I see Mr. Talbot tap the face of his watch a couple times and then make a wrap it up motion. I have to finish watering. I have to organize all the plants that are going to the GSA sale tomorrow, and I'm only half hoping Si will be the one to pick them up. Is that sad?

Bern's expression is sour, like Gia's visit left him in a foul mood. I don't exactly know why. I mean, Gia seeking him out is a good thing, right?

"So, you know," I say, gathering up all our lunch trash, "you and Gia seem to be getting along better?"

He rolls his eyes. "It wasn't that we weren't getting along." He looks more pensive than brooding now, though. He taps his fingers on the table. Finally, he says, "I don't think she really wanted to break up, you know. Neither of us really wanted to break up. It just . . . these things happen, and I guess the problem is that you don't really expect them to."

I swallow down a lump of acid in the back of my throat. Bern's talking about his *feelings*; this is both awkward and terrifying. The burger bags crinkle as my hands tighten around them. "Yeah? So, what, it was just an extended fight scene ending in public humiliation?"

I don't know where this is going, but it kind of feels like Bern is dumping me.

But then half his mouth stretches into a grin. He stands up with a shrug. "Does it matter?" he says. "The end result's the same."

The GSA has two sale spots set up on Sunday morning: one at the vacant gas station at the end of Pine Street, and the other in front of Boot Elementary. There's a mixture of donated succulents and the leftover Easter inventory—a compromise—and we're out there early enough to catch both the before- and after-church crowd.

I'm not thrilled to be there. I got accidentally caught up in the delivery, though, and now I'm sitting in a folding chair between lacrosse sophomore Wart and an unnamed freshman in front of the elementary school, watching Si good-naturedly haggle prices with a couple of smiling blue hairs in matching dresses.

The entire scene is too cute. Si sends me a dorky thumbs-up after the ladies end up with two plants each. I don't understand how that works so well for him. He's got on a backward baseball cap and a Henley with cut-off sleeves. The freshman next to me heaves a dreamy sigh.

We have a giant tent set up so the plants don't wilt in the sun, and it's possibly the most boring three hours I've ever spent on a Sunday morning, and that's including sunrise Easter service. And yet . . .

It's kind of worth it for the way Si shoos the freshman over to the money box and squeezes my thigh as he sits down next to me.

He says, "You're freckling up," even though we're mostly in the shade, and he takes his hat off and claps it on my head, twisting the brim so it's right over my eyes.

I don't even mind that the paintbrush I shoved into the bun at the bottom of my neck falls out, sending a shank of my hair to land messily over my shoulder.

Si tugs on the ragged ends and grins at me.

I clear my throat and wipe my palms as surreptitiously as possible on my pants, thanking the gods that I thought to wear jeans.

Mykos is out by the street in a loud shirt holding up a plant sale sign, singing what sounds like the entire musical score to *South Pacific*. Wart is playing with his phone. The freshman is dealing with a sudden rush of after-church folks, and Si and I should probably be helping her.

It's almost like we're having a moment—I hold my breath, my teeth ache from clenching my jaw, and my arms are numb. Some asshole bird is insistently making itself known in the one huge tree by the parking lot.

And then Si's whole body jerks, like he'd been lost in thought, and he rolls out of his seat and says, "Oh man, Lauren, I'm so sorry," as he moves toward the tables again.

He's still smiling when he looks over his shoulder at me and Wart and says, "C'mon, guys, let's all help."

———

Somehow, some way, I get roped into going out for lunch with Wart, Si, Mykos, and freshman Lauren, who looks like she might pass out from sheer excitement and nerves.

It's easily the strangest lunch date I've ever been on. Not that this is a date. Not that I've ever been on *any* date before. Not that having Wart stuff an enormous cheeseburger into his face across the booth from me while Mykos reconfigures his tomato soup to be 90 percent salt could be considered anything date-like, even if you squint sideways. There are no outward eyes that would think this was a double date with a tag-along fifteen-year-old as a fifth wheel.

Si is squished into my side of the booth. He says, "Wanna help me finish these fries?" even though I still have half a plate of my own.

I have no idea what's happening, but freshman Lauren has started giving me the stink-eye. I want to shout, *You know he's gay, right?* at her, but I feel like that'd just be petty.

Every time Si smiles at me my heart drops into my stomach. Am I leading him on? *Should* I be leading him on? What am I going to get at the end of all this, other than an emotionally compromising Prom with a dude who pity-kissed me?

Because that's what it was. It had to be that. Why else would Bern, who's kept all our touches strictly for show, kiss me in the middle of his bedroom? It'd be stupid to think that Bern actually likes me.

And after Prom is over, he can blow me off as a rebound and it'll *make sense*. That would make perfect sense.

"Nolan?"

I jerk my head up from where I've been blindly staring into the pool of ketchup on my plate. "Yeah?"

Si nudges my arm. "You okay?"

I force a smile and snag one of his fries, holding it up in a salute as I say, "Sure."

Sunday nights are traditionally for family meals. Dinner is a giant pot of spaghetti and garlic boats and a salad full of cranberry "spiders" with Marla dropping enough hints about Bern missing it that I start to feel a little guilty about not asking him to come.

The thing is, though, that I can't shake the feeling that if I hadn't gotten in the way with my *Prom-posal*, Bern and Gia would've eventually gotten back together. It's stupid.

After dinner there's communal TV time and the occasional game of war. Despite its name, war games tend to be the tamest of any Sheffield competition, but they can drag on longer than a Monopoly marathon. Before any kind of war can start, though, we have to decide who's King of the Couch.

"So," Daphne says, eyeing me from the other side of the sofa. The flat soles of our feet are pressed up against each other, our backs against the armrests. We're evenly matched, meeting in the middle, because my legs are spider-long and nearly bent in half, and hers have the strength of ten Scotsmen behind them.

"So," I echo, and I try my hardest not to turn bright red.

"Gia says you met Bern's family."

I slacken a little in surprise and end up with my knees practically up my nose. "What?"

Daphne says, "You heard me," and smugly stretches her legs out to full length, champion of the couch cushions.

"You cheated!" I spring up to loom over her, but she just folds her arms over her chest and grins.

"And you spent Friday night at the Bernsteins'." Her face falls a little. She says, "Which is . . . okay. I mean, it's a little weird that Gia would know before me, since I'm your sister, and Gia is Bern's *ex*."

I sigh, shoving at her feet and dropping back down on the couch. "You're making this a bigger deal than it is."

"Am I?" She crisscrosses her legs and leans her forearms on her butterflied knees.

I press the heels of my hands into my eyes, avoiding her face. "They're still friends," I say.

I feel her squeeze my knee. "Sure. And she totally respects Bern's ability to make his own mistakes."

I drag my palms down my face and peek through my fingers. "You believe that now?"

"I believe anything Gia tells me while shoving me up against the side of her house," Daphne says, nodding.

My hands drop limply to my lap.

"I mean, I could take her in a fight," she says. "But would I really want to?"

This whole conversation is turning bizarre and I'd like it to stop immediately. There's a buzzing in the back of my head warning me that whatever is happening here between Daph and Gia is worse than them battling it out with medieval weaponry.

And then Tom calls from the other room, "Who won King of the Couch?" and, "I made waffle sundaes!" and suddenly I can think about other things, like chocolate ice cream and jimmies, and forget about how my life is probably moments away from falling apart.

Sixteen

Daphne hadn't seen me leave the house Monday morning— she usually isn't functionally conscious until quarter of seven. She takes one look at me as I sit down at our library table for SAP and says flatly, "What."

"Yeah," I say, nodding.

"What is happening? Why do you look like you just crawled out of a dumpster and then got thrown back in?" She reaches out like she wants to cradle my face in her hands, but luckily the table is too wide.

"I had to get up early to bring all the After Prom shit to school," I say. I rolled right out of my bed and into the pre-dawn world, managing to miss both Tom *and* Marla on my way out the door. It feels like something died in my mouth. There's a good chance I'm wearing the tank top I went to bed in under my zip-up hoodie—I can't remember if I changed this morning or not. Am I even wearing under-wear? A casual shift of my hips points to *nope*.

Daphne sighs and says, "I thought we were getting past this." She grabs my hands and says, "You have a new pair of jeans. You have at least three shirts that fit and don't have paint on them—"

"Two," I say. There was an accident. The purple one was sacrificed to the dolphin disaster of last week. I'm using it as a rag now, but there's no need to point that out to her yet.

She jerks upright suddenly, dropping my hands, and says, "Oh my god."

"What?" I ask, sinking lower in my seat.

"Oh my god, Nolan, you don't have a tux." She groans, mashing her head into her stack of prep books.

I bite back the words, *maybe I shouldn't go to Prom then*, because I'm pretty sure she'd stab me with her pen. "I can get one?"

She heaves a deep breath, says, "Okay. Okay, we can handle this. Do you know what Bern is wearing?"

I open my mouth to say *no*, and *probably not a tux*, but she cuts me off with a wave of her hand.

"Never mind," she says. "I'll ask Gia." Like that isn't completely weird at all.

———

I have just enough time to get mints out of my locker after SAP, but not much else.

The lack of underwear is especially difficult in gym, and

I get some shit for jamming myself into a bathroom stall to put my shorts on. There's still a high likelihood of flashing everyone my balls with the hemline they make us work with, but at least I avoid any shirt-snapping of my bare ass. Guys are fucking weird, and gym is a special kind of hell.

I have my hood up and my head down in the cradle of my folded arms in English when Bern shows up.

He says, "This is a new low for you, Grant," with a chuckle.

I flip him off without lifting my head. I'm pretty sure he and Evie are having a silent conversation over me. Probably about how much I smell. I sniff my pits. It's not that bad, but it's also possible that I've wallowed so long in my own filth that I can't be objective about it anymore.

Bern picked a good class to show up for, though, because all Rahm does is put on the first half of *My Fair Lady*.

The classroom is barely even dim with the lights off—the midmorning sun on this side of the building is ridiculously bright—but my eyelids start to droop anyway, my jaw cupped in my left hand. My elbow keeps sliding, and I jerk out of a light doze every few minutes. And then I feel a cool, metallic tickle at my hip—I straighten up, skin twitching.

Bern leans over and says, in a hush, "Are you seriously not wearing underwear right now?"

I'm suddenly and supremely conscious of the way my hoodie's ridden up, sweatpants sagging at my hipline.

Cheeks hot, I grab the end of his pen. "Stop poking me," I say, trying and mostly failing to keep my voice at a whisper.

Mrs. Rahm gives us a pointed look and I twist the pen out of Bern's hand.

When she goes back to her book, I quietly flip open a page of my notebook and write: *I was in a rush this morning*.

The back of my neck prickles in embarrassment at his answering breathy laugh.

The rest of the period lags. I doodle in my notebook, a series of geometric shapes, circles, triangles, pen pressed so hard into the paper that it almost rips. The bell ringing is a blessing and a curse. I tug down my sweatshirt and hitch up my pants as I stand.

I can feel Bern watching me shove my book back into my bag. And then he reaches out and shackles my wrist, sliding his fingers down to fit into my hand.

My palm burns. Suddenly all I can think about is Bern's hands on my face and his mouth on my mouth, and I've been trying so hard not to think about that. To think about how right about now Bern usually drags me into the bathroom, how we'll touch without really touching, and how my skin always tingles when we don't actually fucking make out. I curl my fingers into his and lace them together.

Whatever is on Bern's face can't exactly be categorized as a smile. He tips his head to the side and says, "Ready?"

I have no idea if I am or not, but I say, "Yeah," anyway.

By the time we slip into the bathroom, I'm breathing pretty hard for no other reason than panic and nerves.

Bern takes one look at my face and says, "What's wrong?"

I try to calm my breathing, but the opposite happens. I kind of feel like I'm going to pass out. My "Nothing" is weak, and his hands now cradling my rib cage are not helping. I knock them off with my elbows, but he just moves them to my upper arms.

"Are you having a panic attack?" he says, alarmed.

"No." I might be having a panic attack. I haven't had a panic attack since that time Tom caught me destroying the side of the house. Crap.

And then Bern's grip on my arms tightens and suddenly I'm . . . being hugged. The fog in my brain clears enough to feel one of his hands slide across my back. The lump at the base of my throat expands, making my chest hurt, and then dissolves in a whoosh of stuttering air as I hear Bern murmur, "Hey, it's okay. Breathe with me, all right? You can do it."

I grab onto the back of his shirt, slumping into another breath, and then another, blinking away moisture at the corner of my eyes. Oh my god.

The door opens behind us with a, "Jesus Christ, guys, *must you?*"

Bern says, "Fuck off, Montgomery," his arms still a warm, solid brace around me.

The more even my breathing gets, the redder my face

feels. Wow, this sucks. "I'm fine," I finally say. I stand perfectly still as Bern's arms slowly drop.

He shifts back to look into my face, eyes narrow. "You're sure."

I manage a nod, then rub shaky palms over my heated cheeks.

"Okay," he says, moving even further away. "So what the fuck was that for?"

Grimacing, I say, "No reason?" I think I'm having some sort of mini breakdown. Like my mind can't handle the way I want to kiss Bern, and how he doesn't actually want to kiss me. Like I want more than bros helping bros out, while Bern's on the rebound.

"You had a panic attack—"

"A very small one!" I say, even though all my limbs feel exhausted.

"—for no reason," he finishes.

"We're going to be late for class," I say a little desperately.

"The bell rang five minutes ago."

Fuck. "Look, it was just . . . I was just . . ." I thread my hands through my hair.

"You were just," Bern prompts.

I'm at a loss, though. It's not like I want to vomit up my feelings all over him. I shrug, try to smile.

It must not work very well, because Bern says, "What? Were you freaking out about being alone with me? Is this about Friday night?"

"No!" God, the last thing I want to do is talk about Friday night.

But Bern just looks stunned. He stumbles back a step, and I figure I probably shouldn't have shouted that in his face. He says, "I thought . . . ," and trails off, shaking his head.

He thought *what*, I think. What the fuck is going on between us?

He shoves his hands into his pockets and rocks back on his heels. His grin doesn't totally reach his eyes. "Okay, so. There's a party at Mena's this Saturday. If you want to go."

I heave a deep breath; feel the ache in my chest loosen. "Sure," I say. This is us ignoring the giant rainbow elephant in the room; I can do that. "Okay."

———

School is surprisingly low-key for the rest of the day. The only slightly shady moment comes during art elective, when Zamir prods a somewhat reluctant-looking Bern into a seat at our table. But then Bern grins at me, cocky, and I swallow down acid that makes my stomach feel hollow. Zamir mirrors my awkward nod hello with one of his own, and then the tension gradually bleeds out of me as we all focus on doing another motherfucking still life. The bitch of it is that I think I'm actually getting better at them.

When school lets out, the afternoon is damp but bright.

The sun hurts my eyes, and I cup a hand over my forehead, stumbling a little at the top of the back steps when Evie arrives.

It's Secret Awesome Sacred Art Club day, and I have only two weeks left until Prom. At least I'll be busy with shopping, decorations, and trying to convince Arlo to help me with the giant papier-mâché shark.

"What do you think," I say, when Evie starts down the stairs in front of me, "of asking Rob and Arlo to join SASAC?"

Evie says, "Arlo must beat me in the arena," without missing a step.

"What arena? The tree house?" And what does she want to do *in* the arena? "Is this a battle to the death? Do I have to get Tom involved?" Will there be blood, is what I'm asking, and should I enlist Marla as a field medic.

Evie ignores me and just says, "Can I ask Tamara, too? I bet Bern and Zamir would come."

I pause at the bottom of the stairs. "Wait. Have you *always* wanted to expand SASAC?"

"SASAC is the wind," Evie says. She moves back up a few steps so we're nearly the same height and cradles my face. "SASAC is for all the peoples, Nolan. SASAC is for all lovers of fine art and smoothies. SASAC is—"

"Stop saying SASAC," I say. It's making my right eye twitch. "I get it."

She slaps my cheek lightly. "Good."

"You know, wasn't this whole exclusive thing your fault to begin with?" I say, feeling only slightly bitter.

"I'm perfectly willing to fight any and all comers about Impressionism. Just because Arlo is always wrong doesn't mean I can't coexist peacefully with him after kicking his ass." Her grin is wide, with a worrying amount of bloodthirsty anticipation. "He doesn't *have* to die."

———

The most notable things that happen during the rest of the week are:

I somehow miraculously get an A on my SAP werewolf essay, even though I have no idea what Daphne's grading requirements are. She says she's impressed with my commitment and world building with a look on her face that suggests, perhaps, that the essay was not actually supposed to be about werewolves.

Also: Daphne makes me rent a tux for Prom. It's, uh, extremely red. I'm still not entirely sure how that happened.

And Mim somehow, using her freaky middle-school bewitching abilities, convinces me to sneak into the girls' bathroom with her during Art Buddies on Friday to bleach our hair.

When she ends up locking herself in a stall and sobbing, I figure she's made some sort of miscalculation. I spare a moment for some light panicking about the bright white streak

I've now got running down the front of my hair, and then I rap my knuckles on the metal door separating us.

"Mim? C'mon, it's not so bad." I mean, it could be worse. At least we'll match.

Mim's sobs smoothly transition into something resembling hysterical laughter, so I figure she's not really buying it.

The room smells like peroxide and despair. Evie is going to kill me. I'm pretty sure Daphne will just laugh.

Oh my god, *Bern* is going to kill me. I broke his cousin.

"Mim?" I say again.

She coughs and snuffles and then the lock clangs and the rusted, beige door slowly creaks inward, like in a horror movie.

It's . . . pretty bad. The peroxide dried out and frizzled a solid chunk of her hair—it falls over her eyes in unfortunate kinks, like it's dying and just wants to be put out of its misery.

I carefully grasp her upper arms and stare anywhere but at the limp, piss-yellow lump of hair and say, "We can fix this."

"Can we?" Mim says, "Can we, Nolan?" Her face is red-streaked from tears and she rubs her palms over them.

"This is just step one, remember?" Step two is covering up the bleached blonde with different colors. That we do not have right here and now. It's like a compulsion with us, to do the stupidest stuff we can think of. Mim brings out the complete idiot in me.

I bite my lip, desperately trying to think of something that will help Mim stop crying. Evie's going to start looking for us any minute, since we've been gone for nearly the entire allotted Art Buddies time. "Hats!" I say.

Mim looks unimpressed. "Where are we going to get hats, dumbass?"

I grimace. There's only one thing to do. I tug out my phone and text Evie: *you know how me and mim make terrible decisions together?*

Evie sends back almost immediately: *what did u do*

———

"I'm not wearing this," Mim says, while Bex is hysterical, hiding her face in her hands, collapsed on the seriously gross bathroom floor.

I tilt the feather-covered construction paper hat forward in an attempt to cover the stubborn strand of hair that's making Mim look like a dystopian biker out of an old My Chemical Romance video. "It's just until we can get to a drugstore."

Evie's face is bright red, like she's only holding herself together because she realizes Mim is in a sensitive place right now and doesn't need to be laughed at. More. Since Bex is a lost cause. I'm actually a little worried she might hurt herself, she's laughing so hard, but my first priority is Mim. And how she might start crying again.

"Listen," Evie says, shoving me back with the flat of her hand and maneuvering herself in between us, "this is going to be fine."

I widen my eyes and nod over her shoulder at Mim.

Evie says, "We're going to get some colors. It's going to be cool," with the kind of conviction that actually makes me believe her, too. She jabs an elbow into my gut. "Right?"

I nod my head some more. "Right."

It doesn't help that Bern and Zamir are waiting for us in the hallway when we finally emerge from the bathroom, but Mim holds her head up high.

She says, "Don't," when a goofy grin blooms over Bern's face.

It's painful, deep down inside, how his eyes light up but he doesn't laugh. How they crinkle at the edges when he says dramatically, "Mimsy, what have you done?"

"*Don't,*" Mim says again, but there's a tiny smile at the corner of her mouth now.

We end up at Mim and Bex's house, the whole mess of us, including Bern, and I get a fashionable streak of deep purple while I witness how alike Bex and her mom are—there's more giggling and sniffles and wet eyes as they help Mim create a rainbow.

"This is . . . thanks," Bern tells me as I lag behind Evie on the way out of the house and back to her car. He tugs on my purple streak, grinning. "Mim's a tough kid."

"Mim's crazy," I say. She's amazing. I kind of want her

to help me graffiti Mr. Talbot's greenhouse. In the dead of night, so we can pretend to be rebels.

He shrugs, says, "My entire family thinks you're hilarious now, by the way. They love you, and all you had to do was ruin Mim's hair."

"I didn't ruin it," I say, defensive. I was not the one who showed up at Art Buddies with a container of bleach and a defiant expression. At least he thinks it's funny, though.

Bern ducks his head, a hint of a flush on the back of his neck. I want to press my hands over it, but instead I shove them deep down into my pockets, say, "Okay, well, bye," and walk away.

Seventeen

This is torture. Mid-level circle of hell torture, only with less blood and more rhythmic handclaps.

In some sort of bizarre middle ground between alcoholic rager and spoons, Mena's party Saturday night has managed to settle on a lazy beach vibe without being anywhere near a beach.

Bern is aggressively playing math songs on his guitar in the middle of the patio. All his friends know the choruses of every single one of them, and Daphne is next to me with her hands clasped together, saying, "Oh no," quietly and reverently, over and over again, like this is everything her dreams are made of.

And the thing is, I hadn't really meant to bring Daphne—she'd snagged me on my way out the door and refused to let go—but I'm glad she's here. So she can see this. She can witness what is happening and understand how fucking irresistible it is.

I wish I knew more about geometry, now that everyone is shouting about angles, planes, and dodecahedrons.

Daphne hisses, "This is why you've been doing so good on your math prep sheets," but not like she's upset—more like she's *super impressed*.

I try not to flush too much in pride. Bern is a pipe dream; I'll be back to teetering on the edge of math failure by next year.

I need alcohol to counteract the swarm of bees in my chest. Jesus.

Leaving Daphne to the rousing chorus of "All the baby bears dance to pi times four," I stealthily retreat to Mena's kitchen and its high alcohol content.

Bennett solemnly hands me a red cup that smells like apples and gasoline and says, "Go with god." I assume this either means he's forgiven me, or he wants me to die.

One sip and I feel like I can breathe fire. "Holy crap."

Bennett's face splits into a wide smile. "I know, right?"

"Am I being poisoned?" I say absently, closing one eye and staring down into the murky red liquid. "Did you make this in a bathtub?"

Linz Garber appears out of nowhere and leans into Bennett's shoulder, red-faced and glassy-eyed. She says, "Secrets," drawing out the last *s* so she sounds like a snake and also super drunk.

Taking another sip of lighter fluid or dragon's bile or whatever the hell it is, I lean against the wall and try to look as relaxed as possible. It only takes a few minutes for the alcohol to kick in and almost make me relax for real.

The music is softer this time around. I can still hear the low growl of Bern's voice out the sliding glass door. In the living room, Mena's got a playlist with the Joy Formidable on it, "Cradle" and then "Whirring" giving way to what sounds like early Muse, and then the Sounds. I hum along to "Painted by Numbers" under my breath.

Low-key drowsy, a swallow left in my cup, I stare at the haphazard stack of half-empty pizza boxes. I'm hungry, but not enough to go scrounging, and my arms feel heavy. I blink and suddenly the kitchen is overcrowded, people pouring in from the patio, shaking off rain. I rub a slow hand over my face and then I'm getting jostled into the next room, watching Daphne gulp down a cup of mystery liquid and nearly cough up a lung. I smile, feel all the muscles of my face stretch, tip my head back to stare at the arch in the doorway, and then I'm sitting on the over-stuffed couch, legs spread, shoulder hitched up to a slightly familiar kid that may or may not be from Our Lady, the Catholic school nearby.

My cup is empty now. I frown down at it, nestled into my crotch, but then a full *new* cup slides into it and my fingers curl over the rim to keep it from tipping.

"My guy," Hinkey says, dropping down onto his knees in front of me with a grimace. He palms my thighs, and I'm 90 percent sure he's too drunk to realize how compromising his position is. "My dude, my guy. NGS. Gym bro." He squeezes the muscles right above my knees, and I fight off the knee-jerk instinct to kick him in the gut. "I've seen some things, man. Involving your sister's competitive spirit."

"Daphne?" I cock my head. "Did you let her play beer pong?"

"I'm no snitch," Hinkey says, nodding, and then he leans into me and slowly gets to his feet, knocking the side of my drink with a sly, "Enjoy," before he lumbers away.

"Weird," I murmur, but take a big gulp anyway. It's like my body is learning to swallow flames, or else I've already burned all the nerve endings out of my throat.

Bern is across the room, damp hair curling up, little ringlets falling over his forehead. He's grinning at Gia, of all people, and I can't help but wonder how that happened. Obsess about it. How maybe he holds her wrist a little too long after Mena hip checks her on the way past. My eyes narrow over the way he lets her go, hand hovering until he shoves it into his hair, laugh deep in his chest. This is not the Bern I know. Arguably, I don't actually know Bern at all.

A cold sweat rolls out over my entire body, nausea welling up behind my teeth. I lurch up, using random Our Lady dude as a crutch, and then stumble through the crowd and out the front door. I make it five steps into the open air, sky spitting a light rain, before I'm retching into an azalea bush.

I stay there until I'm left with dry heaves and a pulsing ache behind my eyes. I'm only crying because it's, like, an involuntary reaction to losing all my insides. I've got one knee in red bile, so gross, and then a warm hand presses into the base of my skull.

"You're all right," someone says, voice like honey, and I squint up over my shoulder. The porch light is framing Si's head like a halo.

I try to say, "What are you doing here?" but my brain is raw and all my throat gets out is a rough, hurty *"Buh."*

"C'mon," Si says, carefully hefting me to my feet. "You're gonna feel this tomorrow."

I'm feeling it right now.

My head is half fuzzy, half blindingly clear. I hope he doesn't make me go back inside, because there's no guarantee I'm done puking.

Si helps me sit on the front stoop, though, and then settles next to me.

Water rolls down my forehead, the misty rain layering thick all over me—I lick my lips and swallow hard. I say, "How're you . . . not shit-faced?" as Si grins at me.

"I didn't drink anything made by Bennett and Garber." Si knocks our shoulders together lightly and my palm scrapes the concrete step to keep from tumbling off.

He throws an arm around me and says, "Even your hair looks sad, man."

"I'm not sad." I'm motherfucking miserable. This is

Bennett's fault, and his essence of dragon tears, and also Bern's, and his . . . everything.

Pressing my hands to my face, I groan. I should be drinking so much water right now. So much.

"For real, Nolan, I think Bernstein's looking for you," Si says.

I snort into my fingers. *Yeah, right.* Bern has Gia again, god, he's probably still in love with her, and I have . . . a shaky relationship with alcohol and gravity. With a deep breath, I peek out over my hands. Si has an oddly fond expression on his face, like we're friends, and I feel a glowy warmth in my chest.

Crap. Crap, god, Si is so fucking sweet. He's a marshmallow. I take a deep breath, staring at him unblinkingly. His artfully mussed air, his Hemsworth smile. And I want to be *friends* with him, how fucked up is that?

"Grant?"

I see scuffed black boots first. And then the frayed edges of dark jeans, cut off at the ankles, worn gray at the knees. Bern has his hands in his pockets, a wide-armed tank loose over his chest. My eyes blink slowly, lashes clumped together with rain, and Bern is frowning down at me like he's *disappointed*. What the fuck.

"I'm fine," I say.

Bern's eyes are mostly black, like a demon. He leans close and curls his hands over my elbows, mouth flat. And possibly judging. He probably knows I totally destroyed Mena's front bushes. Ugh.

"Sure you're fine," he says, and then looks over at Si.

Si holds his hands up as I stagger into a position that resembles standing.

Bern says, "He doesn't drink," to Si, like I'm not even there.

Which, first of all—"I don't?"

Second of all, "Fuck you, I can drink." Like, Bern has literally seen me drink before. We played spoons.

Bern scoffs, out loud *scoffs*, which I find offensive, but he's also basically the only thing keeping me upright. I can't feel my knees. My knee bones. My long shins. The things that are supposed to be attached to my ankles.

"Grant? Hey, Nolan?"

I jerk my head up. Bern's eyes have either gone soft, or my vision's gone hazy. "What?"

Bern stares at me, unreadable, but his arms are still around me, and he tugs me closer so that I can lean into his side. He says, soft, "C'mon, let's get you some water, okay?" and leads me back inside.

He says, "Sit right here," and makes sure I don't fall flat on my face while attempting to land on the couch.

He says, "I'm gonna kill Benny," and I pat his arm, his shoulder, his cheek, and say, "Hey, no. Benny's awesome."

Sure, he probably should have warned me I was drinking

pure liquid flames, but you know. I shrug, jostling the mostly passed-out Our Lady kid next to me. Kid and me, together again.

"Okay, champ," Bern says, and I can practically hear the roll of his eyes. He's smiling, though, just a little.

I poke at the corner of his mouth, at a hidden dimple, and he grabs my fingers and squeezes.

"Sit tight, Grant," he says. "I'll be right back."

———

I wake up Sunday morning to sunlight setting my brain on fire. Red bleeds behind my closed eyelids and there's a throbbing in my skull that winds all the way around, like a steel clamp. Whatever was under my bed must have crawled out and died inside my mouth. My tongue feels swollen and raw. Tiny elves are scraping my brain cave with pickaxes, and someone is mowing their lawn outside my bedroom window. My ears are three times their regular size and jammed full with pointy twigs, making my jawbone ache.

I have never felt this terrible in my entire life.

At some point, I manage to crawl my way into the bathroom. I stick my head in the tub, turn on the faucet, and open my mouth under the deluge. My entire upper body gets soaked, but I'm feeling marginally more functional by the time Daphne lurches into the open doorway with a groan.

"Fuck me," she says, voice a hoarse rasp. "Move, god, I'm dying."

She climbs over me, elbows and knees digging into my back, and collapses into the tub like a pill bug, curled on her side and shivering in the shallow water.

"Plug it up and leave me to drown," she says, an arm over her face.

I just turn my cheek into the porcelain and close my eyes, listening to the soothing gush of water.

After a couple of long minutes, Daphne tugs on my hair and I blink open my eyes to watch her finally uncurl. She drapes herself deeper into the tub on her back, pj's already soaked through, then she flicks the stopper closed with a bare toe.

"Bern's friends are assholes," she says.

"How did we even get home?" The last thing I remember is Bern trying to force-feed me crackers. I think harder, risking my brain melting out through my ears. Random snippets of the night come back to me, but the fuzzy image of Bern and Gia, laughing together, touching casually, keeps flashing behind my eyes, and I have to dig knuckles into my mouth and breathe through my nose to keep from throwing up again.

Daphne's eyes are slits over the rim of the tub, and I think her nose might be swollen. She says, "I was gonna call Missy to pick us up, but your boyfriend volunteered." The expression on her still-ashen face could possibly be classified as *mischievous*.

"Oh god, no," I say, cheeks burning. "What did I do?"

"Nothing embarrassing," Daphne says, managing a half-smirk. "Unless you count the way you drunkenly assured Bern you only liked Si O'Mara the way you like puppies." There's a barely there shrug, like her limbs are too heavy. "Which, okay, I didn't think you liked puppies?"

"Who doesn't like puppies?" I say, but also, wow, am I screwed.

She pats my head sloppily. "Don't worry, baby bird, it was cute."

It's not cute. It's too much. It's like I openly admitted to really liking him, while he's obviously still hung up on Gia.

Okay. Okay, time for damage control. I need to call Evie. I need to get dried and dressed. I should probably eat something. You know, when I can move without losing all my insides.

I can hear Daphne's soft snores, and I reach out to turn off the water and unplug the drain before she can drown.

———

My plan is to fortify myself with greasy foods and at least another three hours of sleep, which is why I'm caught so off guard when Bern knocks on our front door.

I hitch my falling pajama pants up on one side,

supremely conscious of the ball of knots my hair has become. My mouth still tastes like ass. There's a throbbing ache over my right eye.

"Uh. Hi," I say.

Bern looks cool and collected, hands in his pockets, sunglasses hooked into the neck of his T-shirt. I stare at them to avoid his eyes.

Bern says, "Well, at least you're still alive."

I dart a glare at his amused expression. "I'm not entirely sure of that," I say, and his mouth inches upward in a small grin. I should thank him for bringing us home last night. For making me drink water and making sure I didn't throw up all over Mena's couch. I remember that much, at least.

Tension creeps up my spine the longer he just smiles at me, like he knows something I don't know. Like maybe I did something worse than proclaim my platonic love for Si. Did I talk about my feelings for *him*? This is so much harder now that I . . . God, I think I really wanted this to be real. Fuck.

Prom is less than a week away, and I don't want to do this anymore.

I take a deep breath as Bern starts saying, "So, about what you—" and blurt out over him, "I think we should break up."

My voice echoes ominously across the yard. I hear a hissed intake of air from somewhere behind me, but my body is locked up, squared against Bern and the bright, high noon light.

Bern looks genuinely confused, brow furrowed. "What? *Now?*"

"I'm just." I make a helpless, frustrated gesture that's alarmingly close to Muppet arms. "You and Gia. I'm pretty sure she'd fall into your arms again if you asked. No fake Prom date from me necessary."

Bern nods slowly. He says, "That wasn't the deal, Grant." He's got Disney prince hair and the wide, brown eyes of a baby deer, skin gilded by the sun.

My fingers itch to smooth over his cheek, and I have to shove my hands up under my armpits. "Isn't that why we were fake dating?"

"No," Bern says, frowning. "Just . . . no."

"Right," I say. My chest feels hollow.

Bern laughs, clipped and unfunny, and says, "Wow, okay. This is not how I thought this morning would turn out. But I guess you don't need me anymore, right, now that you've finally got O'Mara's attention?"

"You—"

"I'm just gonna . . . go," he says, hooking a thumb over his shoulder. He backpedals down the steps, stumbles once before turning around, color hot on his face. His shoulders hunch as I numbly watch him walk back down the slate path to the driveway.

I should probably say something, but I don't have enough breath. It's possible that I'm really, really stupid.

"What," Daphne says from directly behind me, "the fuck," a hand clamps onto my wrist, "was that?"

Fresh off being an absolute dumbass, I twist out of her hold, drag my hands through my hair, and rasp, throat nearly crushed with humiliation, "This is all your fucking fault."

"Mine?" Her eyes are wide, shocked, but with just enough of an indignant edge to feed my anger.

"I can't believe I let you—" But I can, is the thing, because this is Daphne and this is me, and I will always, always . . . I growl under my breath, eyes burning with tears, and push past her, back into the house and all the way through. I slip out the sliding glass doors, over the patio, and disappear up into the tree house, shutting the trap door with a resounding bang.

I expect Marla or Tom. Tom would lure me down with cookies, and Marla would call me sweetheart and give me understanding hugs. They'd do the same for Daphne, validate each of our feelings, and then probably lock us in the den with a pizza.

But I don't get either of them. It's strangely quiet on all fronts.

My righteous anger quickly burns off into boredom, so I crack open Daphne's Saddle Club #6: *Dude Ranch* and read until it's too dark to see. Boredom bleeds into an itch between my shoulder blades, making me uncomfortably tense. I keep waiting for something to happen, but it never does.

Finally, the delicious scent of dinner wafts out the open kitchen window and coaxes me down from my hidey-hole.

Dinner is quiet. Daphne glares at me over her lasagna, and I try to stem the rising panic over how this has never happened before. We've never fought, not really. I clench my fingers around my fork and try to drum up all the frustration and anger I felt before, but I'm breathing too hard.

This is bad.

Daphne and I always get along. It's how our family works. I don't do any stupid shit, and Daphne and Marla and Tom all love me for it.

Tom sends the salad bowl my way and says, "Anything you two monsters want to say to each other?"

I hold my breath.

Daphne says, "No," as she stabs her fork into a carrot.

Tom says, "Fine," and, "Just so you know, I'm declaring this Puzzling Night. Lots of enforced elbow knocking. Get ready to share minimal personal space!"

Marla waves a piece of garlic bread between us and says, "I've got a thousand-piece yellow tulips one I've been saving for a special occasion."

Daphne doesn't even flinch. She just says, "Bring it on."

Eighteen

The painful awkwardness of Sunday night seeps into Monday morning.

Daphne and I ignore each other in the hallway outside our rooms. Or, really, Daphne ignores me, and I try not to feel terrible about it. I open my mouth to graciously offer her first use of the bathroom, only she shoves a palm into my nose, hooks an ankle around mine to trip me up, and manages to skate into the bathroom right before me anyway, slamming the door in my face.

I skip breakfast and bike to school early, grabbing an apple out of the bowl on the counter when Tom gives me the stink-eye.

I narrowly miss getting hit by a Jeep, which lays on the horn as I swerve and skid into the grassy median of the pike. It's so close a call that my nerves are shot, and I shakily jog across the rest of the lanes, and then walk through the parking lot instead of getting back on my bike.

I'm pretty sure this day is gonna suck balls.

Evie is waiting for me by her hatchback, arms crossed and expression dark.

"So you're here early," I say, walking my bike up to her, trying and mostly failing to come off nonchalant. My shoulders feel too stiff, and I'm smiling with entirely too much teeth.

"You got drunk Saturday night," she says.

"I'm allowed to get drunk." Technically illegal, yeah, but not totally against our collective moral code.

She straightens up from her slouch. "You got drunk, declared your epic bro-ship with Si—"

"Please tell me I didn't actually say that."

"—*and*," she presses closer to me, "there's a rumor you broke up with Bern yesterday."

Rubbing a palm over the side of my neck, I say, "I, uh, kind of did."

Evie shakes her head. "I can't believe you. Zamir wants to roast you alive. You know Garber can actually *do* that, right?"

I swallow hard. "Is he . . . is Bern *upset*?"

Sighing, Evie relaxes into my side, curls an arm around my waist. "Upset enough for Arlo to actually *call me* about it. I think Zamir is rounding up a posse. How fake do we think this fake dating actually was?"

"I might be in love with him," I say, faintly horrified by my entire being. *God.*

"Oh man." Evie hugs me tighter. "You're screwed."

My day goes steadily downhill from the second I step into the school.

There's a big hairy dick on my locker, with enough detail and shading to make it the most impressive one to date.

Daphne doesn't show up for SAP, and I spend the time carving a tiny narwhal into the library table with my pen, trying to convince myself that I don't care.

In gym, I didn't realize how much I was starting to rely on Hinkey as an ally until I don't have him anymore. It's only through pure dumb luck that all I end up with are a few scrapes on my knees.

English: There's a bar of sunlight that falls across Bern's empty chair. I space out to the dust motes spinning around it, missing the whole lesson.

I don't know if I can last the rest of the year like this.

Carlos, Dave, and Missy are already at our table when I get to lunch. Dave has *The Idiot* cracked open in the center, and I give him the finger.

Out of the corner of my eye, I see Daphne slip into the lunch room with Gia Hooper on her arm.

I say, "What is happening?" before I can think better of it. I didn't even think Gia had this lunch.

Daphne pointedly ignores our whole table, which is crazy, and tension squeezes all the muscles in my back. I feel like I might crack in half. This is what's happening. Daphne is sitting with Gia and Zamir. My eyes burn and my hands ball into fists, and I can't exactly tell if I'm more angry or hurt.

Missy slams her bottle of water on the table.

I startle and slant her a wary look.

"I don't know what's going on, and I don't want to know," she says. The words *so shut the fuck up* are buried in the way she bares her teeth at me.

Her high ponytail is off-center. There's a strain around her eyes that's usually reserved for Adrian Fells and games of Risk.

"Missy, I—"

She cuts me off with a choked, *enraged* sound, but all she says is, in the voice of the devil, "*Fix this now.*"

———

I don't fix it.

I can't fix anything, apparently, if the murderous looks Zamir is giving me in art class are any indication.

Bern doesn't look at me at all.

From across the room, I notice his hair is flat on one side, there's a sad slump to his shoulders, and he has a smudge of blue paint along his jawbone, even though we aren't using any paints in class. The shadows under his eyes make the back of my throat burn. I don't know what the fuck I'm doing.

The only bright spot is that Arlo and Rob are happy to have their seats back.

Evie says, flicking a finger at them, "SASAC. After school at Nolan's. Be there then or never. Your choice." She makes the choice sound like death, but Arlo says, *"Dude,"* and Rob is making dolphin noises to the embarrassment of everyone everywhere.

We're using colored pencils to draw a red bicycle that's parked in the middle of the room. From my chair, I've got the front wheel turned to the left, the shadow of a pedal between the spokes, the chrome of the handlebars curving down to hide most of the seat.

Ms. Purdy hands out rulers and says, "We're working on perspectives today. Take twenty minutes, and then everybody change seats. Some angles are going to be harder than others."

Evie snorts.

I duck my head to hide a wince. My life has turned into a bad rom-com movie, only chances are slim to zero that I'll actually get my happy ending.

———

It's too hot for this early in May, and the first meeting of the newly expanded Secret Awesome Sacred Art Club starts off with watermelon slices and tall glasses of iced tea on the patio.

It's surreal enough for all of us that we're awkwardly quiet at first. Arlo and Rob are sitting together on the end of one lounge chair. Evie is watching them, stone-faced, from the glass-top table. I'm pretty sure she's just trying to unnerve them for fun.

Normally about now we'd be discussing how weirdly attractive Jonny Lee Miller is, or the healing powers of Lupita Nyong'o's smile.

Finally, Arlo spreads his hands and says, "So do we do art here, or is anyone up for a movie?"

Evie snorts and I muffle a laugh behind my hand before working up enough nerve to ask, "I need help with After Prom decorations, if you're up for it?"

I kind of think they only agree because they think I'll kick them out if they don't.

They're both flipping through my sketchbook when the side gate of the yard rattles. Through the vinyl slats, Tamara calls, "Anyone wanna help a lady out? I've got brownies!"

Rob scrambles up and practically dives for the gate. He swings it wide and says, "Please marry me."

Tamara, grinning brightly, says, "I *also* brought scones and eclairs."

Arlo stares fixedly at the Ground Zero bags she's carrying and says, "Marry all of us."

"Oh, no way," Evie says, rising to her feet. "The eclairs are mine."

"Relax," Tamara strides over and dumps the bags on the table. "I brought enough for everyone." She spins with her hands on her hips and twitches her gaze between Arlo and Rob. "Now. Which one of you is Arlo?"

"Uh," I say, abruptly remembering *the arena* and how Evie was adamant about fighting someone, possibly to the death.

Oblivious to any hand-to-hand combat, Arlo cheerfully says, "That's me!"

Luckily, Evie's duel of choice turns out to be freeze tag instead of fisticuffs. It ends up as vicious as any game played on Sheffield property. My entire shirt is torn down the side, Tamara's skinned both her knees, and Arlo comes out of it with a black eye.

Rob is icing his elbow with a bag of peas and Evie's doling out water bottles when Missy comes stomping into the kitchen where we've all gathered for a cooldown.

We're in the middle of *calmly discussing* how to go about painting the side of Mr. Talbot's greenhouse wall, if we were to paint Mr. Talbot's greenhouse wall, and if we should do it in the middle of the night to feel more like authentic hooligans—Arlo—or in the middle of the day like normal, sane people who don't want to get arrested—Evie—and all arguing stops immediately at the sight of Missy.

Her shirt's untucked and her hair is sticking out on the sides and she glances around the kitchen wildly. I'm behind Rob, pressed into the counter next to the fridge. I keep very, very still, holding my breath, like I'm hiding from a T. rex.

Unfortunately for me, her robot vision zeros in on me in seconds. She says, "You."

I carefully don't say anything in response.

She crooks her middle finger at me and then turns around, stomping back out.

Rob says, "I think she wants you to follow her."

"You think?" I manage around the lump of dread in my throat.

Her head peeks back around the doorjamb and everyone startles back a step, like they're afraid she's going to start shooting laser beams out of her eyes. She says, "*Now*, Nolan."

"Right," I say. "Right, I'll just . . ." I place my water bottle onto the counter, give a salute to no one in particular, and walk as slowly as possible toward the hallway. "See you guys on the other side."

———

I'm not dumb. I know what this is.

Daphne seems to know, too, sitting on the living room couch with her arms crossed, grumpily staring at the blank

TV. Missy glares me onto the cushion next to her, and then stands on the other side of the coffee table to look at us. She seems . . . *concerned*. It's freaky.

"I'm only going to say this once," Missy says, glowering at me and then at Daphne and then back again. She says, "Nolan, Daphne loves you. It's why she's such an idiot about you."

I open my mouth and close it again. Daphne has never told me that she loves me. I've always *assumed* it, we're too close for it to not be true, but it's different hearing the words out of someone else's mouth. Out of Missy's.

She turns to Daphne and says, "Daphne, Nolan is"— she looks visibly pained—"lost without you."

And I get it, I do. I get that this is about Daphne and me, and how we've been fighting and how Missy is freaked out by that, but the greater implication here is that: "You like me."

Missy snorts just a little too aggressively. "I don't give a rat's ass about you, Grant, but Daphne thinks the sun rises each morning just so she can see your smile—"

"You really like me!" I say wonderingly.

Daphne stifles what I'm pretty sure is a giggle.

"I will end you." Missy's right eye twitches.

"You won't." I grin. "Because you like me."

"The matter at hand," Missy says loudly, over Daphne's now less-than-stifled laughter, "is that you're both being morons, so stop it!"

There's a ringing silence. The dead quiet from the hallway probably means that everyone else is listening in.

I watch Daphne's fingers idly picking at the ragged hems of her jean shorts. Her nails are bitten down to the quick. One second drags into ten, into a minute, into ten minutes, and finally Missy says, "Fix this or I will go back in time and make sure neither of you were ever born," and leaves the room.

I drag in a deep breath and say, "You need to respect my boundaries," just as Daphne says, "You *lied* to me."

It feels like a knife plunged into my chest.

I did lie to her. I didn't even . . . I haven't even been thinking about it like that. I lied to her about Bern, about our whole relationship, and somehow just realizing the magnitude of that *right now* makes it all worse.

I say, low, "I'm sorry."

And then she's flailing forward, curling her legs up under her and jabbing her bony knees into my side, being tactile in ways that she hasn't been for more than twenty-four hours, and it's pathetic that I've missed that so much.

She practically shouts, "And how can I respect your '*boundaries*'?" making a face and using air quotes. "You never ask for anything!"

My breath stutters, and my brain goes offline for a long second. Then I say, "What?"

She throws her hands up. "You never ask me for anything. *Anything.* You're, like, passively waiting for me to do things all the time, even hand you the motherfucking salt." Her voice is a low growl. "I have to steal every moment I have with you."

"You . . . don't have to do that," I say, stunned.

"Well, it feels like I do." She heaves a sigh, suddenly deflating. Her whole body droops: hair, eyes, frowning mouth, arms falling limp to her sides. "And then when I'm gone next year I won't even be able to do that."

"You realize," I say tentatively, "you don't have to do anything for me to love you, right?"

"I know!" She threads her hands into her hair, like she's frustrated with herself more than me.

I risk sliding an arm slowly around her shoulders. She slumps into me, palms shifting out of her hair to press over her eyes.

I'm not good with feelings. Neither of us is. That's how we got into this mess to begin with.

"Before," I say, quiet and slow, "I never had anyone around long enough to bother asking for things." My fingers squeeze along her bicep, keeping us both still. "Daph, with you it's not a problem with asking, okay? It's"—my throat is tight and my chest feels heavy—"knowing that I never really had to. You're just . . ." *a force of unstoppable energy*, I don't say. *Larger than life. Amazing, kind, super controlling, crazy . . .* "you."

There's a sniffle from behind us, a faint, "*Awwww*," but I'm hoping if I ignore them they'll all just go away.

That night, Daphne and I lay feet to head in my twin bed so we can both fit.

Tom had emerged from my room earlier with a Shop-Vac and a full black plastic bag with a simple "You're welcome," his voice tinny behind a gas mask. Now the air smells like the lilac plug-ins Marla placed in every single outlet.

Daphne squeezes my toes and says, "You really liked him, though, right?"

I shrug against my pillow. "I might have really liked him," I say. "And now," I leverage myself up on my elbows, "no Prom date." Which is the least of my worries, but at least it's something to focus on.

Daphne gives me a hopeful look. "I know where you can find one."

Groaning, I say, "No more setups, Daph. Haven't we learned our lesson here? And besides, it's too late, everyone already has someone to go with, or they wouldn't have bought a ticket."

"So here's the thing about that, though," she says with a grimace. "They wouldn't let me switch the name on my ticket. I had to buy another one for you to use."

"So all this was, what, a ruse?" I could be mad about that, but what's the point?

"Everything I do is a ruse," Daphne says, waving her hands in front of her face. "I'm ninety percent bullshit fifty percent of the time. I'm handcrafted out of bravado, baby bird, you know this about me!"

There's a single glow-in-the-dark star left lit in the far corner of my ceiling. Fuzzbutt's eyes reflect the moonlight as he watches us from on top of my tall dresser. "Daphne," I say slowly. "You are the most sincere, genuine person I've ever met."

Daphne's indrawn breath sounds watery, and I very carefully do not turn my head to look at her.

I bend my knees and scooch down the bed so I can lace our fingers together, resting my cheek along her shin.

"Daphne," I say, "will you go to Prom with me?"

Her answer is a very quiet, "Yes."

Nineteen

Even though Daphne and I have made up, the days leading up to Prom are dismal. Mostly because Bern refuses to be alone in a room with me—when I can even manage to *be* in a room with him—but also because Hinkey ignores me in gym, Bennett cracks his knuckles meaningfully whenever he sees me in the halls, and Mim is giving me the silent treatment in Art Buddies.

On Wednesday afternoon, after having suffered through an excruciating tissue paper portrait the day before, I break down and hiss, "I messed up, I know it, but you need to talk to me."

Mim just arches an eyebrow at me.

"You're making me crazy," I say. We're painting rocks. Either we talk to each other or I'm gonna throw mine at her head, googly eyes and all.

"I don't know what you want me to say," she says, voice

low. She glances at the station to our right, but Bern hasn't been to Buddies all week.

Sighing heavily, I just say, "I didn't mean for anything bad to happen. Can we please just separate Bern and me from me and you?"

I watch as she painstakingly finishes her rock—black and yellow stripes, like a bumblebee. She drops her brushes into the cup of water and rubs her hands on a rag.

"Do you want me to ask for another partner?" I say.

Her back is still a tense line when she says, "No."

Something in my chest loosens. "Okay," I say. "Thanks."

The elbow she aims at my gut isn't exactly friendly, but I know she could do far worse. She says, "Don't thank me. We've only got two weeks left here, and I don't feel like breaking anyone else in."

———

On Thursday, members of the GSA get permission to skip their afternoon classes to start decorating the gym for After Prom. Si manages to get the entire robotics club to help with the lights. Arlo and Rob finish half of the papier-mâché giant shark—it's better than nothing?—and I buy out all the blue and green streamers at the local party-supply store.

It's . . . not as great as I imagined in my mind. Everyone else seems pretty happy with it, though, so I'm not going to point out how half-assed all the fish are, and how we had to turn the shark so it's just a giant head coming out of the gym floor. Less "Under the Sea" and more *Jaws*, even if Si ultimately vetoed the blood.

Si comes up next to me as I'm watching the janitor and Coach carefully hang the jellyfish lights.

I say, "Did anyone think about how we're going to get them lit tomorrow night?"

Si waggles a remote in the air and then flicks one of the already-hung ones on and off. "We've got all these in a bucket by the door."

I nod.

He looks over at me with his perfectly shaped eyebrows raised. There's a faint shading of blond-brown fuzz all over his face, like he's attempting to grow a beard. I don't even know, that just might kill me.

"What?" I ask.

He wraps an arm around my shoulder, and it sadly does absolutely nothing for me. "Do you want to talk about it?"

"Uh, no." No, I definitely do not want to talk about how apparently I dumped Bern over the weekend. I'm a little confused about why Si thinks *I* need consoling. I mean, I could use some, sure, but everyone's under the impression that this is all my fault. Which it is. I'm the jackass here. Plank called me that in gym this morning, and he doesn't even like Bern.

"Okay, man, but," he leans toward me, hand squeezing my upper arm, "I don't know what happened, but I could tell you really liked him. So if he was pressuring you for any—"

"Oh my god, no," I desperately cut him off. No, no, no.

"I just want you to know that isn't okay—"

"Please, no. Si, that . . ." I shake my head, ducking out of his grip so I'm standing across from him. He seems concerned, pink-cheeked and frowning. "That's not even close to what happened."

He looks like he wants to argue. Like he's really and truly worried about me. He's so competent and hot and sweet. Too bad I'm into deceptively sensitive math nerds.

I say, "You definitely do not have to defend my honor."

He claps my shoulder firmly and says, "You just let me know."

———

Getting ready for Prom is 60 percent sitting on the den couch and trying not to get white cat hair on my red pants while Daphne, Missy, and Evie squeeze into the bathroom and take turns doing their hair. Fuzzbutt is pacing behind me, like he knows I don't want him anywhere near my tux.

I probably should've waited until the last minute to get changed, but they all decided to do *my* hair first. Neatly brushed to a shine, hanging straight past my shoulders. Off-center part, to make my forehead look smaller, showcasing the purple stripe. I feel like a dumbass.

Marla bustles in with a white rose and stands between my knees to pin it on the satin lapel of my jacket. She smooths the fabric with her palms and grins at me.

She says, "You look like you're in a 1980s jazz band." Backing up, she tugs me to my feet. "You played saxophone at Bunny Skylar's wedding. You crushed your solo in *Careless Whisper*, and everyone cried." She reaches up and tucks my hair behind my ears and says softly, "I was so proud."

My eyes burn and my "Thanks" is embarrassingly thick.

And then Tom walks in holding his digital camera above his head. "The dates are here! Huzzah!" he says as Gator and Tamara follow him in.

Gator eyes up my red tux and gives me a finger gun. He's in dark gray and looks like an actual person.

Tamara has on something short, purple, and shiny, a hibiscus bloom pinned above her left ear. Her three-inch heels make her nearly my height.

It's not very much longer before the girls come down—Evie, hair pinned up, dress a matching shade to Tamara's; Missy looking surreally like a fairy princess in pink sparkles; and Daphne, her floor-length gown a deep emerald, so we'll look like Christmas.

"I feel like we didn't entirely think this through," I say when she steps up next to me.

Her hair is fluffed and curly, with a green ribbon tied around it like a headband, ends trailing down her back.

Tom snaps a picture of us and says, "I'm using this for our holiday cards this year!" and then, "All right, everyone in the backyard so I can commemorate this madness and post every single photo on Facebook."

———

The Penn Valley High School Junior-Senior Joint Prom is being hosted in Ballroom B at the Marriott. We give our tickets to Mrs. Rahm, get our names checked off the list, get warned, firmly, about renting a hotel room—how would they even know?—and then pose for the obligatory couple's photo, which I am 100 percent sure will end up in an 8 × 10 frame, hanging on the wall of our den.

Rob, wearing something unfortunate and brown, pounces on the group of us the second we step through the ballroom doors and neatly separates Evie and me from the herd. He says, "Arlo and me had a bet about whether you'd show. I think Linz smuggled in a blowtorch."

"I'm escorting my older sister, which I assure you is not the most pathetic way I could have spent this night." Crying in the bathtub comes to mind. Watching *Dateline* with Tom while eating an entire pumpkin pie. Making playlists that heavily feature Fleet Foxes.

Arlo appears with a full cup of punch and a spring roll tucked into the corner of his mouth like a cigar. He bites into it and says, "Bern's here, too. He came with Gia."

"Awesome." So cool, right? Right. I definitely don't im-mediately scan the room, looking for them.

The place is packed with bright colors, so at least I don't feel like I stand out too much. It's loud, too hot, and I'm hungry, and we probably still have an hour before dinner. I'm already regretting this entire night.

Evie says, "It'll be fine. We'll watch your back. What's the worst Gia can do to you?"

Oh god, I haven't even been thinking about that.

"I think you're okay for now," Arlo says with a shrug. "I'm pretty sure Daphne's her new kryptonite."

"Wait, *what*?" I say, but Evie's got her arm hooked around mine and starts tugging me over toward where Tamara and Daphne have staked claim to a round table.

"Do *you* know what he meant?" I ask Evie.

"I know that Daphne and Gia skipped lunch together yesterday while you were out decorating, and that Missy wants to drown Gia in a well," she says, half absently. She's grinning at Tamara, and how Tamara is dancing by herself at the edge of the dance floor, just past our table.

Never in our entire friendship have I seen Evie dance.

This might be fun.

———

It takes almost all night, surprisingly, for me to finally spot Bern.

He's wearing something dark that sparkles in the revolving overhead lights, slow dancing with Gia, their foreheads tipped together. He's got both his arms around her waist and they're barely swaying. I can see their lips moving as they talk softly to each other, and my face is hot.

Daphne sighs beside me and says, "If you promise not to step on my toes, I'll get you close enough to say hi."

"What good would it do?" I say, still staring at them.

She jabs an elbow into my side. "Don't think like that. You're a catch, baby bird."

"I'm . . ." I turn to look at her, incredulous. "You *have* born witness to the past two disastrous months, right?"

"I think you're somehow missing the glaringly obvious fact that *he really liked you*." She has her serious face on, like she's getting ready to charge the hockey pitch and make an incredibly illegal tackle. "A couple days aren't going to make a difference if you nut up and apologize."

"It might," I say.

"You'll never know if you don't *talk* to him. Now," she holds up her arms expectantly, "are we going to dance? One-time deal, Nolan, I'm not coming back from college next year to be your savior again."

That's a lie. Daphne will definitely come back if I need her. I'm pretty sure, from the wavering half-smile on her face, that she's hoping I'll always know that, now and forever.

"No bumping into Bern," I say, taking her hands.

She rolls her eyes. "Fine. *This* time."

Actual Prom seems surprisingly short.

And After Prom—keeping wound-up teens off the streets from 1 A.M. to 6 A.M.—seems a lot less dumb with all the jellyfish lights blinking from the ceiling and the rotating blue wave light that Si managed to borrow reflecting eerily off the strategically placed lengths of foil on the walls. Two moms, obvious veterans from previous years, are ready with a stack of blankets to give out. One of the dads falls asleep curled around the giant shark head, and the rest of the parents wait it out by napping on and off on the half-folded-up stack of bleachers.

Daphne parts ways with me with a kiss on the cheek just inside the door in pursuit of a high-stakes game of Rummy Royal with Dave, his date, and a bunch of unsuspecting drama kids.

After an hour, I'm encouraged by the sweet delirium of exhaustion to finally go talk to Bern, but of course I can't find him.

After three hours, I wake up in a corner of the room surrounded by beanbag chairs with Evie half on top of me, a low-key headache throbbing in the back of my brain.

Hour four: Everyone gets their second wind. Somebody starts a playlist of what sounds like the entire One Direction discography, and Parker Montgomery the Third streaks through the gym with his tie wrapped around his dick.

It's half past five when I stumble into Bennett. At some point he's changed into PJ pants and a T-shirt. There are sleep-creases on his left cheek, and he's got three bottles of water in his hands.

Overtired and restless, I say, "Do you know where Bern is?"

Bennett looks at me for a long moment. Then he makes a face, hands the bottles off to a shadowy figure inside the beanbag nest corner, and says, "Come with me."

"What, are you going to lure me to my death?" I say, but I follow him out of the gym and into the hall anyway.

We silently walk through the main section of the school, past the admin department and the front entrance, turning right toward the cafeteria, then up the middle stairs and down to the second-floor boys' bathroom.

"Huh," I say, standing in front of the door. The halls are dim, making the bathroom look dark and ominous, but I square my shoulders, push up the rolled cuffs of my sleeves, and take a hesitant step forward.

Bennett shoots an arm out to block me. He says, "This is your third chance, Grant. You fuck it up again and I'll murder you in your sleep."

"Doesn't sound so bad," I say with a nervous chuckle, but Bennett just silently moves his arm out of the way, eyes sharp with warning.

Great.

The thing is, though, that I'm not so sure this even is a

chance. This is just me, trying to explain how and why I fucked up, and hoping Bern doesn't hate me for the rest of my life. I nod solemnly at Bennett, then flatten a hand on the door and push my way inside.

The only light in the bathroom is the gray haze of dawn filtering in through the window.

My "Hello?" echoes off the porcelain, the rusty metal stalls, and the water-stained ceiling tiles. It's empty.

I briefly wonder if Bennett's plan was to lock me in here till Monday, but then I notice that the screen is popped out of the window, and there's a blue tie crumpled up on the sill. Right. It's *this* bathroom.

So . . . out and up. Fantastic.

The sun hasn't quite touched the courtyard below yet. The tops of the two tall oak trees are a bright spring green as the light crests above the roofline. A breeze flutters their leaves and my hair as I stick my head out the window and size up the ragged rope ladder dangling along the brick.

I wrap Bern's discarded tie around my wrist and then reach out for the ladder.

Don't look down, I think, as my dress shoes slip a little before catching on the first limp rung. By the time I make it up to the lip, my palms are raw and there's sweat dripping down the center of my back. When I swing all the way up, rolling flat on the scratchy asphalt, I have to lie there and take a breather, heart pounding with nerves.

"Crap," I say, nearly breathless. "That doesn't get easier the second time."

Silence.

I leverage myself up on my elbows in surprise, hoping that I haven't climbed that magic rope ladder for nothing.

Bern's got his knees up, feet half off the ledge, arms hugged around his legs. He looks young and golden in the sunrise. The light shining through the oak leaves speckles the roof around him. He's . . . I wanna use the word *radiant* here, but even in my head that sounds too lovelorn and too pathetic.

"What are you doing up here, Grant?" He sounds tired.

I almost feel bad about disturbing him, but this is the first time I've managed to get him alone all week.

I hold up my wrist. "I found your tie."

"Good for you." Now he sounds bitter, and I can't think of any way to fix it.

It's 5:45 A.M. I'm on the rooftop of the school with the boy I like. He hates my guts. There's really only one thing to say: "I'm sorry."

Bern is quiet for so long that I'm not sure he heard me.

His "So?" is said to the fire on the horizon, simple but not emotionless. His voice isn't flat or dead, and that's the only reason I risk moving up. Getting to my feet, slow and deliberate, moving down the edge to where he's perched and carefully sitting next to him.

We aren't quite close enough to touch. I've had all week to think about what I wanted to say to him, and I still wasn't sure what that was until this exact moment.

"What are you doing?" he asks, slanting me an accusing look.

"I'm going to tell you," I say slowly, staring down at my hands, "what it feels like to be new. To both a school and a family, and to being, like,"—I curl and uncurl my fingers, watching the bony shift of my knuckles—"gay."

I can sense him tensing up.

"And having a seriously obvious crush on a popular jock," I go on, ignoring the small movement of his hand I can see out of the corner of my eye, "and being teased relentlessly about it."

"Nolan," he says softly.

"It's not—" I shake my head. "It's not really an excuse, okay? I just want to tell you that it really sucked, for a while there, and I didn't realize you weren't even involved in any of that until a couple weeks ago."

"Right," he says. He clears his throat. The silence stretches long and thin, until it snaps with a spill of kids into the courtyard, laughing, formal wear a mess.

My throat tightens, anxious. I say, "Bern, I'm really—"

"So, what, you found out I cried a little when you told me to fuck off freshman year—"

He cried, *too*?

"—and somehow that gave you the idea that I was, what, just gonna use you and drop you? Like we weren't even friends?" His voice ends high and strident enough to catch the attention of a few of the guys below us, but they just wave. One of them wolf whistles. A girl yells, "Bern!" at the top of her lungs and tries to throw a shoe at us.

"No. No, I'm saying I'm *sorry* for that. I know it doesn't really help." My shoulders are stiff and my shrug is forced. "I thought you really wanted Gia back, and I didn't want to fuck things up for you again."

He's staring at me, I know he is. I can feel it. When I risk a glance at his face, his eyes are wide and his mouth is parted in surprise and he says, "You're a fucking idiot."

I lick my lips. I feel like I swallowed a ball of thorns; there's a prickly pain at the top of my chest. My nerves are making my feet numb. "I really like you," I say, bold, and also on the verge of panic.

He doesn't blink. "Why?"

I could say anything here. I could say it's because he saved me from humiliation with the Prom proposal. Or because he has tattoos, drives a motorcycle, and always insists I wear a helmet. I could say it's because he loves math, and math *songs*, and is sweet to his little cousins. How he still cares about Gia, even though she broke his heart. How he drove Daphne and me home from Mena's party, and fed me water so I wouldn't die. Because he helped me with

Daphne's insane SAP homework and let me meet his parents and doesn't seem to care that I was an asshole about SASAC and Ms. Purdy and Arlo and Rob. I could say it's because of how the sun on his face makes his eyes look nearly black and his mouth this deep ruby red. The soft breeze lifts the slight curl of his hair, brushing it across his forehead. He's really hot, okay, and I won't say it's a stupid reason to like him, but it's also not really the main one.

Instead of any of that, though, I let the silence drag on long enough for him to sigh. To shift to the side and push himself to his feet. His body is framed by the gray-blue sky on the other side of the sun, tall and wonderful.

"Just because!" I shout out as he turns away.

He freezes and looks back at me.

I swallow and go on: "I like you just because I do, okay? There are too many reasons to count right now, and I'm not good at feelings."

"You're . . . not good at feelings." There's a small twitch at the corner of his mouth.

I scramble up and take a step closer and he holds his ground. I say, "I've never been in a relationship before."

"I don't think you're in one now," he says, but his whole body relaxes. Shoulders sloping, weight shifted into his hips.

I move so the tips of our shiny dress shoes are touching. My hands and fingers ache, pulsing in time with the beat of my heart. "I want to try."

"Are you asking me out, Grant?" he says.

I can't really read his tone, so all I say is, "I don't know, am I?"

He's smiling a little fuller now. He says, "Maybe you should figure that out."

Bern is nearly the same height as me. At some point I'll hopefully grow into my shoulders and arms and thighs, and maybe we'll be the same width, too.

I shake my head. "I have," I say. "I mean, I did. I am." And then I kiss him.

I won't say it's the single scariest moment of my life, but it comes close: I frame his face with my hands, even though he doesn't move toward me; I tilt my head, and close my eyes on his still open ones, curious and passive; when our lips touch, his mouth is stuck on the half-grin. He doesn't back away, but he doesn't give in to it either.

I pull back after that dry pass of a kiss and drop my hands to my sides, shaky with the sudden release of adrenaline. I did it. That just happened. It's like relief, terror, happiness, and dread coursing through my body all at once.

"Okay," he says, voice suddenly hoarse. His smile is softer, and he reaches out to swipe a thumb across my bottom lip. "Yes."

My belly swoops and I surge forward to kiss him again. He cradles my jaw, other hand on my hip, hot through my dress shirt. Teeth nip my bottom lip and I shove my hands into his hair, swallow his grunt when my fingers get tangled. He tastes like pizza and lemonade and I forget to breathe through my nose. After what seems like forever and an instant, I fall away, panting, and he turns his head into my neck, damp breath making all my limbs tingle.

Exhausted, I lean into him, hands dropping from his head to drift down his spine and settle around his waist. We're hugging, basically, and it's pretty much the greatest feeling in the world.

The school will be closing up soon.

Everyone'll be going home to sleep for the rest of the weekend.

My stomach grumbles and I say to the side of Bern's head, "How do you feel about waffles?"

Twenty

I don't think I'll ever get used to riding on the back of a motorcycle, but it might be fun to try.

Bern pulls up to my house and parks behind Daphne's piece of shit car. He cuts the engine as I release the death grip I had around his waist and tug off my helmet. I almost fall trying to climb off the back, but he catches my arm and I lean up against his side.

It's early enough that Marla might still be asleep, but Tom'll probably already be cooking. Daphne's either hitched a ride home with some friends or one of the minivan-driving parental chaperones.

It's sunny and cloudless out, and our front lawn is still in shadow, misty steam rolling off dewy grass from the rising heat of the day.

Bern slips off the motorcycle much more gracefully than I did and hooks his helmet in between the handlebars. He's still in his tux, a starry sky navy—rumpled, dress shoes scuffed, tie haphazardly stuffed behind a pocket square. His shirt's unbuttoned past his collarbone.

I stuff my hands in my pockets, suddenly awkward. I want to slip off my jacket, flip it over my shoulder, and coolly invite him inside. I want to do this knowing that in all likelihood Daphne is already at the table, ready to challenge me to a bacon-eating contest.

Bern's silence is unnerving, though, even if his mouth is still red from kissing.

"It's not that big a deal, right?" Meet the parents, yummy breakfast. I don't even have any intimidating aunts or uncles or grandparents or cousins. Just Tom and Marla and Fuzzbutt. Clasping his arm, I say, "You really only have to impress the cat."

Bern shoots me a look I'd like to think of as fond, but I don't know all his looks yet. "The cat."

"And, okay, this is really important." I tug on his arm until he turns to me fully. "Tom's gonna ask you if you want ice cream or strawberries on your waffles."

"Okay." Bern nods, squares his shoulders like he's going into battle.

"The correct answer is yes."

His eyebrows furrow in the middle. "Yes."

"Yes," I say, boldly moving my hand down his arm to lace our fingers together.

Marla will call him sweetheart and Ira instead of Bern, probably, and at some point Daphne'll pass out facedown in her half-empty plate, hair in the butter. Tom will have fortifying tubs of at least three different kinds of ice cream, a hot and ready waffle iron for any second and third helpings, and orange juice, strawberries, and bananas to keep us from getting scurvy.

"And you—" He stops, squints an eye shut, mouth pulled up on one side, like he's having some kind of seizure. Then: "You really want me to come in."

"Well, yeah," I say. We're dating now, right? The real kind, where P the 3 actually might walk in on us with our hands down each other's pants. That could be fun. "We're having breakfast." Tom always says waffles are the most important meal of the day.

"Nolan," he says, but I can see the secret dimple at the corner of his mouth, the threat of his smile.

My thumb sweeps over the back of his hand, and I bounce a little on the balls of my feet, suddenly more confident. Breakfast, nest in the living room with a bunch of afghans and pillows, nod off to the soothing narration of *House Hunters International*.

"Waffles, Bern! Waffles, napping, lawn games, outdoor movie tonight, a midnight graffiti run at Talbot's, possible paintball war tomorrow." I'm pretty sure that's what Daphne has planned for everyone, deep in the woods around the reservoir, where we will potentially all end up arrested. Good times.

"All right, Grant," Bern says with a small, soft laugh. He gestures with our joined hands down the front path. "Let's go."